SILVERGLADE

THE DREAM

WORKS BY
RICHARD LEWIS GRANT

The "I LOVE TO READ" Series:
SILVERGLADE ~ THE DREAM
SILVERGLADE ~ PEOPLE OF LIGHT
GOLDENROD ~ SECRET HOPE
GOLDENROD ~ MYSTERY
GOLDENROD ~ DARK OF THE NIGHT

APS HOMESCHOOL SURVIVAL GUIDE

THE READING GATE

SILVERGLADE
THE DREAM

❧

Richard Lewis Grant

APS PUBLISHING
A division of
Advantage Preparatory Schools, Inc.

Silvergade - The Dream. Copyright © 2007
by Richard Lewis Grant
Published by APS Publishing®
A division of Advantage Preparatory Schools, Inc.

Cover photo: Richard Lewis Grant
Cover design: Mariann Geiser
Photo of author: Christopher Glenn Photography

Printed in the United States of America

Library of Congress Control Number: 2007906550
ISBN 978-0-9798062-0-9

To order additional copies of this book please visit:
www.Amazon.com

the online store at:
www.APS4me.com or

BookSurge, LLC (866) 308-6235
www.booksurge.com
orders@booksurge.com

Dedication

To
Brandon Lewis Grant
and
Brittany Nicole Grant

My dearest children,

     You were there so many years ago, lying in the big bed, fighting sleep, wanting more stories. Once Quasar and Nemo appeared, nothing else would do, not Lewis, not Tolkien – only your very own Quasar and Nemo. How many nights I ended with "and what happened after that I'll tell you tomorrow," having no clue what would happen next. I spent countless lunch hours and commute time imagining what indeed would happen next. And now, putting ink to paper, Silverglade is ready. Thank you for sharing Quasar and Nemo with the world.

I am the most fortunate of dads

Richard Lewis Grant

Acknowledgments

Telling bedtime stories is one thing, making them into books is quite another. Many hands and hearts have helped turn the original "Adventures of Quasar and Nemo" into

"Silverglade ~ The Dream", "Silverglade ~ The People of Light", "Goldenrod ~ Secret Hope", "Goldenrod ~ Mystery", and "Goldenrod ~ Dark Of Night".

Though a complete list would be much longer, I would especially like to thank:

Cindee Grant, how many versions of the same page is a wife supposed to read? Thanks, you read them all.

Dave and Kathy Enos, editors extraordinaire and friends.

Michael Enos, for loving Silverglade and wanting to know what happens next.

Mariann Geiser, your graphic skills are almost clarevoiant.

Pam and Mark Collins, you read the first version at Forest Home, and encouraged us to keep going.

Linda Hollingsworth, your patient review and corrections were so very helpful.

Fritz Ridenour, thank you for your tutelage in the profession of Writer and for your friendship.

The kind **parents** from Advantage Preparatory Schools (APS) who acted as focus groups and provided comments and encouragement.

The kind **students** from APS who, as one voice, kept wanting more. Yours was the best encouragement of all.

My late mother, **Odette Nicole Grant**, who taught me the love of books and the enjoyment of imagination.

Blessings,
R

Table of Contents

CHAPTER 1
The Dream

*E*ven in the darkness of the cave, the darkness of the night, the darkness of deep sleep, Nemo felt the shadow pass over him; a momentary evil that briefly stirred him in his sleep and then was gone. By the light of his fire's glowing embers, Nemo quickly surveyed his small shelter. Everything seemed to be as it should be, and yet something was wrong. He could feel it.

Silently, Nemo put on his shepherd's cloak and took up his staff. He was thin and tall for his sixteen years. From a distance, he might almost be mistaken for a full grown man, but manhood had not yet fully come to Nemo. When it did, he hoped his beard would be as dark and curly as the hair on his head.

Nemo slipped out of the cave to interrogate the night and to protect his flock. Instinctively, he knew he was already too late. When the morning counting was completed,

Nemo was sure more of his sheep would be missing. It was not uncommon for a shepherd to lose a sheep or two. After all, protecting the defenseless fluff balls against attacks by wild animals was a big part of what shepherds do. But this was different.

Normally, evidence of a kill was easily found. A shepherd would find tufts of wool caught in the brush or bushes crushed by panicked sheep. There might be the trail of a dragged carcass, the paw prints of the attackers, or perhaps even blood. It all spelled death to a shepherd. Even the youngest shepherd could follow such trails to the remains of an unfortunate animal, and there were always remains. Even in the worst famine, some parts of the carcass could still be found. Legbones, hoofs, and bloody wool were never consumed, even by a starving wolf pack. Now, however, things had changed.

When these new disappearances first started, Nemo thought of thieves. Very good thieves, he had heard, could steal an animal without making a sound or leaving a trail. But after checking with others in the area, he was sure it was not the work of ordinary thieves. Many ranches had lost sheep; all had vanished without a trace.

Thieves would have to make a mistake at some point, but none had been discovered thus far. No one had yet found their trail. No unfamiliar horses had been seen. No one was selling unaccounted for sheep. No extra wool was in the marketplace. No strangers had been seen in the quiet township for months. And perhaps the greatest mystery was the number of animals missing, and the distance over which the crimes had occurred.

Nemo and his best friend Quasar had each lost sheep, many sheep, so together they began checking other flocks. At first, the boys imagined some plot against them by the adult owners.

"Maybe somebody's jealous," Nemo had wondered out loud as they rode to a neighboring ranch.

"Jealous!" replied Quasar. "Of what?"

"Well," Nemo had said, trying to put words to his thoughts. "We're young and we already have ranches and flocks of our own."

Nemo had laughed outloud at the thought

and then said, "They can have the sheep, just give me back my family."

It was true that no one had ever owned ranches and flocks at such a young age, so perhaps someone did begrudge them their success. The fact was, Quasar and Nemo had paid dearly for their land and livestock. They each had lost their families and had each survived, alone, to inherit the land. There was no plot against them. There just couldn't be.

When their families died, the others in the valley had been kind. Many had given them food, some had even given them lambs and, more importantly, knowledge. Years of experience had been passed on to the boys who now had no fathers to teach them. Why whould these same kind friends steal from them?

"Besides," Nemo reminded himself as he stepped outside his cave, "every shepherd around here has lost sheep."

The fact was, dairy farmers had reported cows missing. Villagers had reported horses missing. Everyone was missing animals, all with the same report: The animals disappeared without a trace.

Nemo wrapped his cloak tightly to block the pre-dawn chill. He stood outside the little cave, listening, trying to hear anything that would warn of danger. Nothing. All he could hear was the bleating of his sheep.

Slowly, Nemo walked down the steep rocky trail to where the sheep were sleeping — or should be sleeping. Already he could see they had scattered. Some had found their way up the trail almost to his cave. But why? What had frightened them?

Again, he stopped to listen. All was quiet. Very, very quiet. The night sky was clear, dotted with a tapestry of starlight. The Ancients said that stars sang. If only these stars would sing him a song and tell what they knew of this danger.

Unexpectedly, the hairs on Nemo's neck prickled. A shiver ran its course down his spine. Nemo's crystal blue eyes flashed left and right looking for anything that would explain his sudden fear.

Nothing. All he could see was the familiar shapes of brush, boulders and trees, muted in the star-lit darkness. As he carefully surveyed the hillsides, he felt he was being watched. He knew he was not alone.

cs　cs　cs　cs　cs

"And what about 'nother for me?" wheezed the old man as drinks were passed around. "C'mon," he whined, when no one answered, "how 'bout juz one more?"

"Not if you're not paying for it," growled the inn keeper. "You've had enough if you have no coin."

The old sailor looked around the small dark room. No offers came for another free drink, only laughter, curt snarls and jeers.

The light of the fireplace and from the few small lanterns that graced this closet of an inn was not enough for his old eyes. Yet, he knew their faces. He could smell their grins, feel their pity. It was time to leave. Turning away he stumbled for the door.

They fed him and gave him drink each night because he was an old sailor and they all were seamen, too. But they had never sailed with him, never fought with him, never mourned with him. The food and drink was a limited fraternity. He was a sailor, but not a shipmate.

"I don't need you, you sea filth," he cursed.

"Get out of here then," shouted the inn keep, with practiced rage.

It was the same each night. He gently grabbed the old man, slipped a potato into his vest, and feigned throwing him out the door. A man needed pride as well as food and drink.

Slowly he picked himself up from the hay and mud. "Always a soft landing, God bless 'im," mumbled the sea dog.

Slipping his hands into his vest, he warmed them on the roasted gift. It was the last warmth his hands would know tonight, for he had no gloves.

Blending into the fog, he walked seaward. Home was a driftwood shanty, cold, drafty and damp. He would eat his feast alone and in the dark. A blanket made of discarded sail canvas would keep him dry and reasonably frost free.

Stopping at the alley that led to his hut, the old man turned his head and listened. Icy fog whipped his crevassed face, and the air was heavy with sea-salt. He took a burdened step or two and stopped again. Ear inclined to the sea, he heard, no, felt the danger.

His back stiffened as he turned from home and ordered his feeble legs run to the jetty. "Cursed old bones," he panted as his feet shuffled to the water's edge.

By the time he reached the rocky barrier that protected this town from sea-rage, the old man was faint and breathless. His heart drummed an irregular tattoo. Onward he pressed, over the boulders near shore, onto the slick moss-covered breakwater.

"I'm in luck; tide's out," he said as he smiled to himself.

The old man's sea legs took him farther out than many a younger man would dare in daylight. Finally, he stood still and listened. Waves crashed dangerously near. Spray soaked through to his skin and fog encased him in a gray shroud. There was nothing, but still he waited. He knew. In his bones, in his blood, in his feeble heart, he knew.

❧ ❧ ❧ ❧ ❧

"More lard," ordered the first mate.

His whispered command was immediately obeyed. Each oar-joint was greased, wrapped in cloth and greased again. With the oars thus muffled, the oarsmen pulled in silence. Even the drummer's cadence was canceled.

"They've done this long enough," ordered the first mate. "The beat should be in their heads by now."

So it was, and they pulled silently as one.

"Where's that lard," hissed the first mate.

"Coming, Mr. Schooper," answered the cabin boy.

He struggled from the galley with the hot iron pot. Being the youngest and smallest cabin boy in the whole fleet, he always worked the hardest.

He started below, his arms aching from the weight of the pot. But in his haste he slipped and fell. The pot clanged against a metal bar, spewing hot grease on deck and below. The poor lad tumbled into a row of oarsmen.

Their rhythm broken, the men released the oar and helped the boy stand. It was a mistake. Their great wooden oar crashed against the one from the row ahead of them as the rowers pulled a new stroke. The men groaned, the ship creaked.

"Clean up this filth," ordered the first mate,

holding in his temper. "And grease those oars," he added, needlessly. He shook his head and looked to shore, trying to hide the embarrassment his son had caused him.

⊂⊃ ⊂⊃ ⊂⊃ ⊂⊃ ⊂⊃

The old man's head jerked toward the sound of the iron pot echoing across the water. Then he heard the sound of oar upon oar, wood crashing, cracking.

"Thar be no mistakn' it," he cried, and redoubled his vigilance.

He heard a young voice cry out in pain. And then, as if by command, the fog lifted for a moment, and he saw them.

Ship upon ship, upon ship, upon ship. Warships all they were and fully armed. An armada greater than the ancient mariner could ever have imagined emerged from the gray mist. From the mast of the flagship there flew a mighty flag; twin black hawks on a field of gold.

The shock of it caught his breath. Then the vision was gone, fog again cloaking this silent floating threat.

"Alarm," he cried with the voice of his youth. 'To arms, to arms."

The old man turned to shore. He alone could sound the warning; he alone could save the town. He must save Mecenas.

"Hurry, Hurry."

Then one foot caught on a rock, the other slipped and he went down hard. The pain came suddenly like thunder. Grasping at his chest he tore open the soggy tattered vest. He willed himself to stand, pulled at his foot, now locked under wet stone, and collapsed again.

Pain. Monstrous, hideous, all consuming pain.

"Catch yer breath," he told himself. "Jus catch yer breath." The ragged seafarer pillowed his head on a seaweed covered slab, and watched helplessly as his small spud of a meal rolled out from his vest and bounced off the rocks into the chop.

ଔ   ଔ   ଔ   ଔ   ଔ

Nemo pulled up the sleeves of his cloak to free his arms, and tucked the lower parts into his belt to free his legs. If danger was near, he wanted to be ready to fight or maybe flee.

Without warning a strong hand reached out from behind and grabbed him by the shoulder. Twisting violently Nemo tried to strike with his staff, but too late. Strong arms pinned him from behind. In vain he struggled against the rock-hard muscles of his captor. Sheep bleated their protest and scattered in fear of this abrupt commotion.

"Be quiet," whispered a voice. "You'll wake the dead."

"And you will join them, if you don't let me go!" returned Nemo.

He tried to strike, again in vain. Rocks and a small cavalcade of dirt plummeted from the path to the fields far below as two sets of feet struggled savagely near the edge of the cliff.

ℳ ℳ ℳ ℳ ℳ

The ships, fifty in all, slipped silently past the harbor. Only one pair of eyes had caught a glimpse of the armata and they now saw no more. High tide would be in by dawn. Before anyone missed him, the old man's body would be washed out to sea. In a few days, perhaps a week, the inn keeper would notice his absence. Some inquiries might be made. No one would know his fate. In time, oh so little time, a squall would claim his hut for the sea, his face would be forgotten, and none would remember his name. Few knew it even now.

Rounding the point just past the harbor entrance the ships caught favorable winds. The flagship, *Fyrmatus*, unfurled her mainsails and shipped her oars. The sails caught and filled, the mast groaned, the bow wave grew and churned white. Soon she was streaming under full canvas. Each ship in its turn followed suit.

"Mr. Schooper," shouted the captain from the quarter deck.

"Sir?" answered the first mate, glad to be under sail again.

"Please order the crew on deck and tell the oarsmen to rest."

"Very well, Captain," answered the first mate and turned to go below.

"Mr. Schooper."

"Sir."

"How is your son?" asked the captain, failing to hide the concern he felt.

Captain Lewis was kind and fair. He treated his men well and expected excellence in return. The crew never failed him. Never. Like his father and his father before him, Captain Lewis was a fine sailor, an exceptional Captain, a good man.

Standing like this, on the quarterdeck, with a stiff wind and full sails, he could still hear his father's voice.

"You can control men by fear and a dose of the whip or you can lead men by example and a dose of praise. The whip is faster and easier, but remember this: men will do greater deeds for honor, love and respect than they will ever do out of fear and pain."

In this, as well as in everything else, Captain Lewis rowed in his father's wake.

"My son, sir?" asked the first mate with calm detachment. Too calm. His heart quivered. He had hoped no trouble would come to the lad or to himself. But if it came, he knew he would have to take the punishment for his son.

"Don't be a fool," he reprimanded himself. "The captain's a good man."

Still he was afraid. He had served other

captains whose tongues could cut as deeply as any whip, and whose whips were never still for long.

"How are the burns, Mr. Schooper?"

Captain Lewis had looked in on the boy just moments before coming up. He was more concerned for his new first mate than for the lad. He needed Mr. Schooper to trust him, unconditionally. Such trust is earned, not ordered. "It takes time," the captain reminded himself. "Be patient."

"They're not as bad as we first feared, sir," he replied, breathing a long low sigh. "Thank you for asking. My son will be just fine, sir." The first mate looked up intently at the captain, waiting.

"He's a good lad, Mr. Schooper."

"Aye, sir. That he is," he said, chancing a smile.

"How long 'til the fleet is in position?" asked the captain.

"With this wind, about an hour, an hour and ten, at the most, sir."

The first mate spoke as accurately as he could. No need to pad the estimate, as he might have done with other captains, lest he be caught short.

"I shall inform Lord Norrom, if you are certain," said the captain quietly.

"Aye, sir. About an hour, if the wind holds, sir."

"Carry on, Mr. Schooper. And please give the oarsmen my compliments. They worked hard."

"Aye, sir," answered Mr. Schooper and he disappeared below.

Within seconds crew members began taking their positions on deck. All knew their jobs, all knew what was expected of them. They went to work, immediately, without a sound.

"They're a good crew," Captain Lewis said to no one. The quarter deck is a lonely place. Then, taking a deep breath, he prepared to give his report to Lord Norrom.

"He's young," he said to himself as he passed his temporary quarters and stood before what normally was the captain's door. His cabin was now occupied by a man less than half his age.

"Young Lord Norrom has not had time to learn all that his father wants to teach him. But," he reminded himself, "Young Lord Norrom is the Admiral."

"Come," came the cracked voice in response to his single knock. It was the voice of youth. "Come," came the voice again. This time deeper, louder, with practiced assurance. Captain Lewis took a deep breath and opened the door.

"Yes?"

The captain was surprised to find Lord Norrom smartly dressed in full battle gear, save for his weapons, dark blue cape and cap, which were normally stowed in a tiny closet near the door. He was sitting at the captain's large oak table, on which were spread numerous charts and maps. The room blazed with light. Every oil lamp was lit and he had two extra lamps anchored to the table itself. The captain noticed that the portholes were darkened and sealed with thick black cloth. Not a single ray of light escaped.

"What is it Captain?" asked Lord Norrom, quietly. He did not look up from his work.

"If the Admiral please," began Captain Lewis. "I'd like to report that the fleet will be in position in about two hours, sir."

Lord Norrom slowly set down the calipers that he was using and raised his head. Piercing blue eyes, not unkind, seemed to search the captain's very core. He brushed his ample blond hair back away from his face.

"Please come in, sit down, Captain," said Lord Norrom smiling politely. "May I offer you a drink?" he asked, taking a flask and two small crystal glasses from a nearby tray.

"Oh, no, please, Lord Norrom," answered the captain with equal politeness. "I don't want to disturb the Admiral."

"Let us toast to a safe landing," said Lord Norrom pouring a thick reddish liquid into the glasses. The crystal sparkled bright red. He stood and handed a glass to the captain.

"To a safe landing," intoned Captain Lewis touching the lip of his glass to the lip of Lord Norrom's. An incredibly clear, pure tone filled the room.

"To a safe and silent landing," smiled Lord Norrom and then downed the drink in one fluid motion. The captain did likewise.

He was surprised at the taste. It was full flavored, but neither strong nor overpowering. It had no bite and was lightly sweet with a kiss of exotic fruit.

"This is delicious. If I may say so, sir," said

the captain, unconsciously running his tongue over his lips. Lord Norrom smiled slightly. "I have never had it before. May I ask what it is, sir?"

"No, I would guess you have never even seen it before." replied Lord Norrom casually.

A momentary shadow passed behind the captain's eyes.

"Captain, I meant no insult," continued Norrom with a warm smile. "It's just that few, outside my family, have ever seen it, much less tasted it. It's a family secret, made only for the House of Hiram by the House of Hiram."

"I wasn't insulted at all, sir," answered Captain Lewis, quickly.

"In the old tongue it is called "Saine Tourkue," said Lord Norrom, watching the captain carefully. "Enemy's Blood," he added with a grin. "We only drink it before battle. It is a tradition."

"It is an honor to drink with the Admiral," declared Captain Lewis, loudly.

"Please Captain, sit down, won't you?" Lord Norrom motioned to a chair opposite his own. "I was just looking over these charts. Perhaps you would be good enough to show me exactly where we are."

"Yes, of course sir," answered the captain.

Perhaps I have misjudged the young admiral, thought Captain Lewis, pleasantly. He scanned the charts and quickly pointed out the location of the fleet.

"I believe we are right here," he said pointing to a place on the chart. "We'll arrive within two hours, sir."

Lord Norrom picked up the calipers he had been using when the captain first entered the cabin. He inserted one end directly under Captain Lewis' finger and proceeded to walk the instrument across the chart to a place where a star was drawn.

"Two hours, Captain?" asked Lord Norrom dryly as he looked up from the chart. "By my calculations, we shall be there in no more than one hour. One hour, Captain."

"Yes, sir," replied Captain Lewis immediately. *How could you be so stupid*, he chided himself. *You misjudged him all right*.

"Our mission is critical, Captain. Landing these troops quickly and quietly will complete the first phase of my father's plan. Long has he labored for this moment."

The young admiral stared intently at Lewis. Beads of sweat glistened on the poor man's forehead.

"When all is ready "Captain, "the House of Hiram will move against an evil more terrible than you can possibly imagine. There is no time to waste. We have much to do, Captain Lewis," continued Lord Norrom.

The captain quickly stood. "Aye, sir. Much to do, and one hour in which to do it, sir."

"The long boats must be made ready and the troops fully armed and on deck before we arrive. I want the first wave launched the moment the tide turns. Is that clear, Captain?"

"Aye, sir. Very clear, sir." *The young Lord Norrom can teach you a few things, you old fool*, thought the captain.

"Signal the other ships. All must be ready in one hour. We shall have two hours of darkness after that in which to land. Then, the fleet must sail for the horizon. By sunrise, we all must be gone, with no visible trace on land or sea. Do you understand, Captain? No trace on shore or sea."

"Yes, sir. I understand, sir," answered the captain.

Only his long years in training kept his voice from trembling. *How could you be so stupid?* he thought, again.

"Look at this, Captain," ordered Lord Norrom quietly. "We have thousands of men already in place here," he said, proudly.

Pointing to the chart he continued, "It has taken months to get the men in place. They traveled overland in small groups, posing as merchants, peddlers, and tradesmen. Their wagons were full of the provisions and equipment we will need."

Captain Lewis stared at the chart as if he could see the secret troops.

"The hardest part was disguising the war horses," continued Norrom. "Anyone can tell a charger from a wagon-puller. That's why we landed the cavalry by sea."

Lord Norrom noticed the captain's surprise at this last revelation. It had the desired effect.

"Yes Captain," said Lord Norrom, smiling. "We have landed here before. I know you understand, Captain, that secrecy is of the utmost importance. I captained those voyages myself."

"Yes, sir. Of course, sir," answered Captain

Lewis somewhat lamely.

Pointing to the coastline on the chart and drawing a line inland Norrom continued,

"The men have cut a path from this bay to this valley. The lines of defense are already in place around it. The main tents are already erected. Everything is ready. Our army will disembark and disappear in two hours. High tide will even wash away our footprints in the sand."

"Admiral, I was not informed," began the captain.

"No, you were not," interrupted Lord Norrom.

He was pleased with the captain so far, and didn't want the man to damage his career with a careless word under pressure.

"You were told to sail the fleet to a certain position by a certain time and a certain day. You have carried out your orders perfectly. Well done, Captain."

"Thank you, sir," answered Captain Lewis. Forty years at sea and that was the only thing he could think of to say.

"The fleet will harbor here, Captain," continued Lord Norrom, pulling out a chart from a wooden tube that lay next to his chair.

He pointed to a small island about an hour away from their current position. "This island is not on your charts, Captain."

Captain Lewis, speechless, blinked hard as he examined the new document.

"Please, don't be offended, Captain," said Lord Norrom as he poured another round of Saine Tourkue.

"Knowledge of this island, like the rest of our plans, is a tightly guarded secret. Apart from the House of Hiram, you are the third to know of its existence. Plus, of course, the men who are stationed there." Lord Norrom handed the glass to the captain, who still stared at the new chart.

"We have men there, too?" asked Captain Lewis as he accepted his drink. "Thank you, sir."

"More there than we have on board. But let's not talk of them. Let's drink to the brave men we have right here. Besides, if all goes well, by dawn you will be on the island yourself."

ᑣ　ᑣ　ᑣ　ᑣ　ᑣ

Nemo glanced over the edge of the cliff.

The darkened view of the rocks below gave him extra strength. He pushed mightily with both legs in a futile attempt to spring away from this human prison. Twisting his body back and forth, he tried to break free. He wildly thrashed about with his staff. It struck a boulder and vibrated painfully from his hand. Nemo groaned as he dropped it. "Now what?"

"Brother, forgive me. I did not…" "I did not mean…" I did not mean to scare you," a voice whispered in his ear. It panted with the effort of restraining Nemo.

"Why then are you out here, hiding on my trail?" roared Nemo. His fear had turned to anger.

"I have come to help you," the voice whispered. Slowly the vice-like grip that held Nemo relaxed.

"How, by stopping my heart?" Nemo turned to look full in his friend's face.

Even in the darkness, Nemo could see Quasar's mane of wavy blond hair and his dark eyes, wide with concern. Nemo's anger turned to laughter as he saw his friend.

"I didn't almost wake the dead, I almost joined them," said Nemo, with a smile. But his smile was cut short as Quasar's strong hand again clamped over his mouth.

"I did not run here before dawn just to scare you. Be quiet. Be careful. There is danger near," Quasar whispered.

Nemo abruptly remembered why he himself was out so early. He remembered his sheep, the cows, the horses. He picked up his staff. Again he felt the danger.

"Why are you here?" asked Nemo in a voice so low that Quasar could barely hear him.

"I sensed danger, evil," answered Quasar. "I could not sleep, so I climbed up to my roof to enjoy the stars and wait for morning. I was watching the stars over your lands when they seemed to disappear, like a dark cloud blocked them from my view. It was only for a moment. I thought perhaps I was dreaming. When it happened a second time, I knew you needed my help."

The boys climbed onto a large flat boulder that jutted out over the trail and the pastures below. They sat and talked. The peaceful panorama of charcoal sky, deep purple mountains and grazing sheep contrasted with their mutual, unnamed dread.

"I, too, could not sleep," said Nemo.

He told Quasar all about his dreams of the evil shadow. As Nemo spoke, darkness retreated from the dawn.

Quasar was a couple of years older than Nemo, broad shouldered and taller than his friend. He wore a green home-spun shirt, laced in front with leather strips, and full length britches. The pants, like his heavy black boots, were bought in the village, something of a luxury he could well afford.

In years past, Quasar had bested Nemo in everything. Now, however, as they both navigated adolescence, the difference in age became less and less apparent. Quasar and Nemo often spent hours talking and working together. They had been good friends even before their families were killed. Then their hearts were woven together by common grief.

Quasar shivered as he listened to Nemo.

"It was dark and so big it blocked all the stars. There was this putrid smell, like a carcass left in the sun to rot. The smell of death. It was evil. I knew this thing wanted to kill me. Then I opened my eyes. I was in the cave, dreaming."

Sunrise chased the morning dampness and warmed the still, frosted air of dawn. As he listened to Nemo's dream, however, Quasar could feel only a cold, overriding sense of dread. Shadows remembered from last night's sky surfaced in his mind. The more Nemo spoke, the more uneasy Quasar became. It was all much too familiar.

The amazing thing was that much of Nemo's dream was somehow already familiar to Quasar. Even before Nemo spoke, Quasar could picture what his friend would say.

"I know it sounds as cracked as Old Simon's clay pots," said Quasar with a forced smile, "But I saw part of your dream while stargazing from my roof. I saw what you dreamed. I, too, felt the danger. I too smelled the putrid scent of death. But I wasn't sleeping."

Nemo didn't answer. He looked at his friend to make sure this was no joke. Quasar's bright smile had dimmed, his laughing eyes were solemn. Quasar wasn't joking. Anyway, it was too early for jokes.

"I have to get the sheep," was all Nemo said.

Together the boys moved Nemo's flock to the high pasturelands. This place was highly prized. It was said that Spring came there first. Actually it was sunlight that came there first. The surrounding mountains sheltered the valley from harsh winter winds, yet let in the first rays of morning light all winter long. In summer, shadows from these same mountains gave shade from the hot afternoon sun. The early morning light helped the grass grow lush and green, even in winter. Frost seemed to leave there first in spring and return there last in winter. Even in the driest summer, morning dew jeweled the pastures and kept them moist. It was called Silverglade.

Silverglade was envied by all who knew of it, loved by any who had visited it, and cherished by Nemo and his flocks. Best of all, hidden deep within Silverglade, at the very place where two mountains touched, was a translucent blue lake. Fed by mountain rivers and natural springs, the lake was always full and clear. In winter it rarely froze, in summer it was never dry, and in spring it filled with delicious migrating fish called ponta.

Even this morning ponta could be seen

swimming upstream. Quasar and Nemo brought the sheep to the upper pasture near the lake. As the sheep began to graze, a welcome peace lulled the boys to silence. Nemo was the first to speak.

"About two years ago, a man came to my house. He said he knew my father." Quasar noticed the tone in Nemo's voice. It was a mixture of awe and anger.

"Who was this man? What did he want?" Quasar knew this was no idle talk. Nemo barely whispered the answer.

"He wanted Silverglade." Nemo struggled to continue, his voice filled with emotion. "The man offered me gold, horses, anything I wanted."

"Why didn't you tell me this before?" Quasar was amazed. They had known each other since before they could talk. In all that time, Nemo had never withheld any secret from his friend.

"You do not understand," said Nemo after a moment of silence. "This man is wealthy, very wealthy. He brought a leather bag full of jewels and poured them out on the table before me. 'Just a partial payment,' he told me."

Nemo shuddered as he spoke. "The man

had long white hair and cold blue eyes. He offered me more riches than I would have ever dreamed possible."

The boys were silent, each afraid of what might be said next. Finally, Quasar faced Nemo.

"Well?" he said with feigned lightness. "Is my best friend, now, a wealthy man?"

"No, no of course not!" Nemo's voice trembled. *How could you even think I'd yield?* His mind screamed, *Don't you remember we scattered our parents ashes here?* But he only repeated, "Of course not."

Nemo started pacing. He always paced when he thought he'd done something wrong.

"Don't you understand? The trouble I am having, the trouble we all are having, I have brought it upon us. The man said he would not rest until he had the land. He said my father had showed him Silverglade years ago and had almost accepted his offer then. I am sure, from that day on, the man purposed to have it." Nemo was almost shouting now.

"My father refused him, and now my father is dead; your father is dead; our families are dead! The man is killing the sheep, the cows, the horses.

Perhaps next he will kill..." Nemo felt his friend's strong hand on his shoulder.

"He will kill no more." Quasar's voice was firm. "It is time to go to town," he said with quiet resolution. "If he is so great, someone there will know where we can find him."

CHAPTER 2
The Road to Town

*Q*uasar always felt uncomfortable in town. The closeness of the buildings, the noise, the strangers all combined to make him feel uneasy. Today the feelings came upon him much sooner than usual. Shortly after crossing First Bridge, Quasar became quiet. Usually quick to laugh or speak, today Quasar only spoke one or two words at a time, and only in answer to a direct question.

"Why are you so quiet today?" asked Nemo.

Quasar didn't answer.

"What are you thinking about, or should I say, who?" laughed Nemo.

Still there was no answer; Quasar just glared at his friend.

Their silence was broken only by the staccato sound of hoof on cobble stone as they rode across Second Bridge.

By the time Quasar and Nemo crossed Third Bridge, a veil of silence totally shrouded Quasar. Even Nemo's wit failed to penetrate the barrier.

"So, brother, will you try to see the baker's daughter?" Nemo smiled to himself. The mere mention of the baker, let alone his daughter, was usually enough to make Quasar blush. Today, Quasar was deaf to it.

"If you see her, will you speak to her? If you speak, do you think she will answer?"

Nemo was beginning to enjoy this game. He had momentarily forgotten the reason they were going to town. He loved teasing Quasar about Brittany. Never before had the game gone this far. Normally, long before this Quasar would have said something or if possible, thrown a rock or a stick. Today, he didn't even throw a warning look.

"What do you think she will say? Perhaps she will give you some bread. Perhaps she will ask you to dinner. I insist on coming." Nemo laughed out loud.

"I cannot possibly leave you alone with a girl so forward as to ask a man to dinner. How can a father let a girl like that go unaccompanied on the street? Why the baker himself must be..."

Nemo was enjoying himself so much he didn't notice his friend no longer rode next to him. Looking over his shoulder, Nemo saw that Quasar had stopped in the middle of the road. He turned and rode back.

"I'm sorry, Quasar." Nemo was humbled, now that he had hurt his friend. "I shouldn't have said what I did. Forgive me, please." Still he didn't answer.

Quasar hadn't heard a word of it. For almost half a mile he had focused on a large encampment south of town. Nemo followed his gaze. Who had built it, and when, was certainly a mystery to them. They were sure it hadn't been there when last they came to town.

"What will the town gossips have to say about this?" wondered Quasar aloud.

Even at this distance what little could be seen of the compound was impressive. By looking carefully over hills and through forest trees one could see, flying above the camp, a strange standard: twin black hawks on a golden field. Quasar had never seen nor even heard of such a flag. Nemo forgot all about his little game. His memory returned full force.

"Quasar," he said quietly. "We have found the man."

At last Quasar spoke. "How can you be so sure?"

"Look, can you see his standard?" asked Nemo. "Twin black hawks on gold."

It was barely visible, but they could see enough.

"The man who came to me wore a cloak clasped with a golden pin," said Nemo. "On the pin were twin black hawks, just like those."

"I know you said he was wealthy, but I had no idea how wealthy." Quasar stared wide-eyed.   "This is the camp of a king. And no small kingdom at that! He travels with a full army."

"I am sure he has more than we can see," answered Nemo.

Suddenly, swiftly, five men, fully armed and on horseback, surrounded the boys. They had been hiding, watching and waiting in the woods that bordered the road. Their horses were carefully armored with leather aegises on necks and flanks. All five carried swords, bows, and arrows. They wore handsome forest green uniforms of light wool with jackets and caps of tooled green leather. Their caps were engraved with a golden shield and twin black hawks.

"Why do you block the road?" demanded one of the men, his nostrils flared like a war-horse eager for battle.

"Why do you stare at our camp? Are you spies?" shouted another, his eyes narrow and harsh, "The Lord Hiram has many enemies."

Quasar looked at the man who had first spoken. His jacket was lightly finished in gold trim. He seemed in charge of the others. Perhaps he was a junior officer.

"General," said Quasar lowering his eyes. "I am but a shepherd and did not mean to block the road."

The soldier remained silent.

Quasar looked up and said, "But it is the free road, is it not?" His words were cloaked in humility. "We are just traveling to town on a simple errand."

Nemo stared in amazement. He wanted respect from this guard, who was certainly not a general. He wanted to shout: "We are not mere shepherds. We own our own flocks and land. We even have hired men of our own," but he remained speechless.

"Forgive me for staring," Quasar continued slowly and quietly, "but, I have never seen such splendor. The Lord Hiram must indeed be great."

The guard looked carefully at Quasar who was unarmed and indeed had the look and smell of a shepherd.

"On your way, farm boy," commanded the guard gruffly.

Quasar smiled to himself. His humility had worked. They would soon be in the relative safety of town.

Suddenly, another guard drew his sword and blocked Nemo's path with his own horse.

"I have seen the silent one before," hissed the man, pointing his blade to Nemo's chest. "I traveled with the Lord Hiram to a farmhouse one day's journey from here. This one opened the door. I do not know what took place inside, but when we left the Lord Hiram was very angry."

Nemo knew he should answer, but his speechless lips were frozen. All he could see was the pointed blade. Light seemed to dance off the sharpened edge of the sword. Nemo wanted to say something, but his mind was empty .

Quasar took a deep breath. Gone was his small humble voice. In its place was a voice calm and sure. "As you know, the Lord Hiram's anger is awesome to behold, and terrible to feel."

Quasar sat erect in the saddle and spoke loudly, boldly. The guards looked surprised at the transformation. Quasar gazed steadily into the guard's eyes, his face a mask of poise. The man glanced away, momentarily.

"As this guard has said," continued Quasar confidently, "my friend has entertained the Lord Hiram, *personally.*" His voice hung on the last word. Quasar turned in his saddle to address all the soldiers. "If my friend has had business with your Lord, is it wise to risk his anger yourself?" he asked.

The men looked at one another in alarm. None of them answered. The soldier nearest Nemo lowered his sword. "It's working," thought Quasar.

"We shall be on our way," said Quasar sharply. "We will be sure to remember you to the Lord Hiram when next we see him."

Quasar kicked his horse forward and the guard who blocked the path gave way. Nemo followed.

"One moment, young sirs," commanded the officer, as he fitted arrow to string, calling the bluff.

"If you are indeed friends of the Lord Hiram, he would be grieved not to see you. You would not have me risk his anger for lack of hospitality, would you?" asked the officer, in mock humility.

Quasar and Nemo looked grimly at one another.

"Let me extend an invitation to you in the name of the Lord Hiram."

The soldier's voice was cold and hard. To guarantee the "invitation" was accepted, several bows were made ready, and swords were drawn. The soldier in front of Quasar turned his horse, blocking the way to town with mount as well as blade. The others formed an arch on the left side of the boys. They were blocked in front, behind and to the side.

Quasar looked to his right; escape into the woods was impossible. They would be shot before riding halfway to the trees. There was no way out. Quasar forced a warm smile.

"How could we refuse such a gracious request?" he asked, panic rising in his throat like bile.

Nemo finally spoke. "You," he nodded to the guard with the sword. "Inform your good Lord Hiram that Nemo, Lord of Silverglade, and his Counsel, Lord Quasar, are pleased to accept his kind invitation. Be quick about it!"

Nemo was fortunate that his voice did not tremble like his heart. The guard mistook Nemo's prior silence for confidence. Yielding, he looked to the officer. Receiving a slight nod he returned his sword to its sheath, turned his horse, and galloped toward the camp.

"This way my Lords," said the officer with calculated deference.

The man did not believe that Quasar or Nemo were lords. But if they were, his career was already at risk. It would not be wise to add insult and risk his head as well. He decided not to bind them. However, to let them escape meant certain death. Therefore he kept his arrow at the ready. With it he pointed the way to camp. As they set out, the officer and a guard rode in front, the other two behind. They all held their weapons at the ready.

Quasar and Nemo carefully slowed their horses and fell back a little from the front guards. They hoped to speak, unobserved. Without looking at Nemo or moving his lips, Quasar spoke quietly. He was pale and even though it was not hot, sweat glistened on his forehead.

"Nemo, Lord of Silverglade?" He still couldn't believe the words. "And his Counsel, Lord Quasar!" He nearly spat the words.

"It was the only thing I could think of," smiled Nemo weakly, not daring even to glance at Quasar.

"From now on," insisted Quasar, forcing a smile for the benefit of the guards, "Let me do the talking. And please, follow my lead."

As if he had suddenly lost his mind, Quasar began laughing loudly. A little slow to understand the charade, Nemo finally joined in the laughter. *It is going to be a strange day*, he thought.

The distance between the front and rear guards increased as the group neared the first perimeter sentries. The front guards paused and spoke into the air:

"These lords have business with the Lord Hiram himself. Passage requested."

Two men emerged from the bushes holding bows at the ready. The sentries were hidden in the young forest that grew nearest the road. They too wore forest green and had netting woven with sticks and grasses covering their jackets. Nemo hadn't even noticed them until the front guards had spoken.

Movement and quiet noises revealed sentries in all directions. The two who now stood on the path seemed to recognize the guards, but nonetheless, they visually searched Quasar and Nemo, stripping them with their eyes.

"Passage granted!" announced one of the sentries.

With these two words, Quasar and Nemo entered Lord Hiram's world. The little group kicked their horses and continued the journey.

Now that they were within the first perimeter the five guards seemed to relax a little. This gave the boys new freedom to talk and make their plans.

"We must negotiate the sale of Silverglade," whispered Quasar. Nemo was shocked.

"Never" he said, a little too loudly. His fiery eyes warned against betrayal.

Quasar glanced at the guards and laughed out loud, then resumed his line of reasoning.

"We must pretend to negotiate." He spoke quietly, soothingly, trying to calm his friend. "It will do no harm to talk as long as no agreement is made, and no gold exchanges hands."

"I will never sell Silverglade," hissed Nemo, under his breath.

"You don't need to sell it, just talk about selling it."

Nemo nodded, "I understand."

"Nemo, listen to me." Quasar's voice was urgent. "Nemo, you must not accept any gift, whatsoever. Do you understand?" Nemo nodded, but he didn't really understand. He was still thinking about losing Silverglade. Quasar glanced at the front and rear guards. They looked bored and unconcerned. He then grabbed Nemo's arm in his vice-like grip.

"Listen to me," said Quasar sternly. "Nothing can be allowed to give the Lord Hiram an excuse to take Silverglade by force. Don't you see?" Nemo was beginning to understand.

"If he wants to take Silverglade he certainly has enough men to do it," said Nemo bitterly. "Combined, our workers and friends would be outnumbered a thousand to one." Nemo paused and looked around at the guards.

"Not only that," he continued "these soldiers are experts at killing. Just look what they did to the sheep."

Nemo shuttered at the thought of the slaughtered animals. "What difference does it make what I do?"

Quasar looked at the guards. They seemed to have relaxed, talking carelessly as they rode.

"Nemo, think with me," said Quasar. "If he wanted to, the Lord Hiram could use this army to take Silverglade and the entire township as well. But he would need an excuse."

Quasar looked intently at his friend, then continued. "If you take a gift, he could later say you had accepted it as earnest money for the sale of Silverglade. Then it would be his word against ours. With his honor at stake, he would simply move in with his army."

It began to make sense to Nemo. He looked to Quasar and sighed helplessly.

After a moment Quasar whispered, "If we are to leave tonight with our honor, Silverglade, or even our heads intact, we must be careful. Very careful."

CHAPTER 3
The House of Hiram

*T*hey were led into the camp from the west. Whether by design or convenience this path took them directly through the tented barracks. Smoke from a hundred fires hung lazily in the still air, stinging their eyes.

The barracks were erected in a meadow, behind a knoll. They were invisible from the road. As they rode, tents spread out before them coloring the meadow like rainbowed mushrooms after a Spring shower.

The entire area was well fortified. Quasar and Nemo had passed no fewer than five sentry posts, each constituting a concentric circle of defense. The boys were in awe of such military might; they had never dreamed of such power.

Finally, they passed through the inner defenses. They were an unbroken bulwark of felled trees, iron spikes, trenches, and thickets positioned at the base of a steep hill. The guards stopped and looked up the path. Quasar and Nemo followed their gaze. Down the incline rode three horsemen.

In the lead was a man of some import. He wore a bright red cape lined in gold. If the boys had ever seen such finery, they would have known the cape was silk. His uniform was unlike any Quasar and Nemo had yet seen. Like the cape, the uniform was red with gold trim. Woven into the very fibers of the breastplate were overlapping golden metal disks. Each disk bore an imprint of the twin black hawks. On his head the man wore a great plumed chapeau. Even his horse was adorned in plumage and red leather coverings.

The second rider was uniformed in sky blue. Like the others, his cap was engraved with a golden shield and twin black hawks. This rider carried a curved golden horn.

The third rider was dressed in white and bore a large flag; the twin black hawks on a gleaming golden field. It was the standard of the Lord Hiram himself.

"Who is that?" asked Quasar, masking his alarm.

"Lord Hiram's son," whispered the

nearest guard.

All the guards sat erect on their horses. No one spoke. The horseman in red released the guards from their task with a nod. The guards lowered their eyes and proceeded back toward the barracks.

Quasar noticed a look of fear had come upon the junior officer who had captured them. Apparently, he had not expected them to be well treated at all. Instead, these "farm boys" were met by an honor guard led by none other than Lord Falcon, eldest son of the Lord Hiram!

Quasar hoped the soldier would not be punished. "I bet he is sorry he started this whole mess," thought Quasar. "But not as sorry as I am." He laughed to himself.

"You, you there! What is your name?"

Quasar couldn't believe it. He turned to see Nemo shouting and pointing at the soldier. "So much for following my lead," he sneered silently.

"Me, sir?" answered the guard. "My name is Hogan, sir." A slight tremor in his voice betrayed him. His eyes widened in fear.

"To whom do you report?" continued Nemo, "Lord of Silverglade." He seemed to be enjoying his new status in life. Quasar wanted to shout, "Enough. Leave him alone!" but, he did not.

The man paled and visibly shrank in his saddle. The Lord Falcon turned full-faced toward the soldier. His eyes narrowed dangerously. Like a fog, silence hung thickly around the men.

"I report to Captain Balworth, sir."

Hogan felt his career being cut to shreds. He never imagined that these two really were lords. He looked for a moment to Lord Falcon and then back to Nemo.

"Well done, Hogan!" said Nemo, loudly enough for all to hear. The shock nearly knocked the poor man from his horse.

"Please give my regards to Captain Balworth," continued Nemo smiling broadly.

"Yes, sir!" returned Hogan, smartly.

Lord Falcon nodded, smiled slightly, and spurred his horse. It would not do to keep his father waiting. He spoke no greeting, made no comment. After turning from Hogan, Lord Falcon gave no warning, but urged his horse up the steep path on which he had appeared.

Quasar sighed heavily, for the day was still

young and sure to be full of such surprises. "Let's go," he whispered to Nemo. They quickly followed the three riders.

Lord Falcon, his standard bearer, and the signalman rode beautifully, fearlessly. It seemed as if they flew over rocks and brambles. They and their horses rode as one, a powerful pas-de-deux of muscle, speed, and daring. Even though Quasar and Nemo prided themselves as horsemen, it took all their skill to keep up with the others. If they had not, their charade would have ended before it began.

Lord Falcon leaned heavily into a turn, rounded it and disappeared past the curve in the path. Quasar and Nemo were falling farther behind.

"Come on!" shouted Quasar. "We've got to do better than this."

He kicked his horse again, and swatted Nemo's as he passed him. Rounding the curve Quasar was surprised to find that Lord Falcon had left the path. He was riding so recklessly through the forested hillside that the plumage flew from his hat.

Quasar and Nemo followed Lord Falcon as

best they could. Brambles scratched their arms. Branches reached out to dismount them. Still onward they raced.

Without warning, they came upon a forward military encampment. Workers, all dressed in deep purple, assembled huge machines of war, ramps and wheeled towers. Men climbed trees and swung from ropes in mock battle. Swordsman dueled in practice combat. The entire forest was alive.

Lord Falcon never slowed his pace. All activity in the encampment stopped as he approached and rode on. The soldiers stood erect in his honor and in honor of the golden flag. Everywhere they looked Quasar and Nemo saw military might and splendor. It was a feeling they would long remember.

Without cue or warning the signalman raised a golden horn to his lips and blew a flurry, crisp and loud. Never once did he slow his pace or break stride. His signal was answered by a signalman some distance away, and then by another, and again by yet another, still farther away.

"What do . . . " "what do you . . . " "what do you think..." began Nemo. The quick pace of the ride left him breathless and he needed all his wits to keep his seat. Even if he could have spoken, it would have done no good. What it all meant was a mystery to Quasar as well as Nemo.

As the path leveled out Lord Falcon slowed his horse and finally came to rest at the crest of the hill. Quasar and Nemo arrived only a few moments later. Lord Falcon still had not spoken. Nemo wanted to ask many questions at once. Fortunately, he caught sight of the downward side of the slope and it rendered him speechless.

The main camp was in full view. Not a tenth of the camp could be seen from the town road. The largest pavilion, so majestic at a distance, was immeasurable closer-up. It was surrounded by ten large and beautiful tents and hundreds of lesser tents. The large tents were all shining in the sunlight and all flying flags made of various colored silks.

The great white pavilion flew the flag they had already seen, twin black hawks on gold. The ten flags on the other tents each had the same crest, twin black hawks, but each had different colored fields. The tents matched the colors of the ten flags. One was blood red, one fire orange, one bright yellow and another shimmering silver. These four were grouped around one side of the great pavilion.

Another was dark blue, one sky blue, one deep purple and yet another the color of wine. These four were erected around the other side of the pavilion. Directly in front of the great pavilion were two other tents. One was forest green, and one striped with the colors of all the other flags, including gold. It was so grand Quasar and Nemo could only stare in mute awe.

If the boys had been observant enough, they would have noticed the lesser tents that were clustered around the ten large tents. Each small tent shared the color of a larger tent, some red, some orange, some yellow. At first glance it was all colorful, all beautiful; but there was planning and order in the splendor.

The tents extended around the main pavilion like great colored spokes in some massive wheel. Neither Quasar nor Nemo noticed it. The amount of activity, the number of people, the number of horses and the glory of it all staggered the boys.

The Lord Falcon did not speak or move.

Clearly, he was waiting for something. Nemo remained speechless. He knew he should say something, but his brain could not find the words. Finally, Quasar found his voice: "The half has not been told. Your father's majesty is without equal."

This small courtesy was apparently sufficient. Lord Falcon glanced at the signalman who immediately blew another flurry, different from the first. The effect shocked the boys more than anything they had seen so far. All activity below ceased entirely. All noise stopped as the echo of the trumpet faded. All eyes turned upward toward the hill. It was as if the world had come to an end.

Lord Falcon nudged his mount forward. Slowly, the honor guard descended the hill, followed by Quasar and Nemo.

"Well, my Lord Nemo. This will be a story to tell our children," whispered Quasar full of fear and wonder.

"If we live long enough to get married," answered Nemo, without a smile. His throat felt suddenly parched and tight.

Their ride ended before a tent, some distance from the main pavilion. It was nondescript except that it, like all the tents around it, was bright red. The standard bearer and the signalman both disappeared without comment or command. Activity throughout the camp resumed. Quasar dismounted and stood quietly with Lord Falcon, but Nemo sat like a stone monument. When a young boy came and took their horses' reigns Nemo recovered his wits and dismounted.

"I am Lord Falcon. My father will see you at sunset."

Lord Falcon spoke simply, yet there was power in his words.

"You may freshen yourselves in this tent. Appropriate clothing, equal to your position, has been provided."

There was no sarcasm in his voice.

"When you have finished, if you would like, you may tour the camp. I will return for you here shortly before sunset. Please, do not be late." Lord Falcon was polite, neither more nor less.

When Lord Falcon left, Quasar and Nemo found themselves alone in a large tent. Hanging from ropes were various sets of clothing; beautiful, colorful, lavish. Within the tent sat two huge vessels made of bronze. These tubs were full of water, steaming hot and scented. As politely as possible, it seemed, Quasar and Nemo had been asked to take a bath. Apparently, the smell of sheep was not acceptable to The Lord Hiram.

"I don't want to take a bath," said Nemo looking at the steaming vapors.

"I don't think we have a choice," whispered Quasar. Nemo touched the water, removing his hand quickly

"This is so hot it could boil eggs," whined Nemo.

Before Quasar could answer, the sound of jingling chains and tinkling bells invaded the tent. Turning around quickly, the boys were met with the last sight they expected to see. Two beautiful girls, about the same age as Quasar and Nemo, had entered the tent.

The girls were modestly dressed in multi-colored silks and adorned with gold chains and silver bells. Each wore a short red cape. Their long hair cascaded down their necks and swirled around the edges of their capes. One had shiny black hair, the other was golden blond. Neither

Quasar nor Nemo had ever seen anyone so exquisite, so exotic, so lovely.

Quasar, who had begun to disrobe, quickly put on his shirt. The girl nearest him, the one with black hair, giggled.

"We did not mean to startle you," she said with a disarming smile.

Her skin was milky white, offset by raven black hair. Her large round eyes were as piercingly blue as Nemo's.

"My name is Leah. Lord Falcon sent us to help you with your bath."

Nemo was speechless. He didn't want to take a bath, and he certainly didn't need her help. He looked at Quasar and then back at the girls. Leah took a step toward Quasar.

Nemo noticed that each girl carried a shallow basket containing soaps, oils and sponges. The blond girl moved closer to him. He retreated away from the tubs, away from the girls. His head began to spin. From somewhere in the back of his mind Nemo heard Quasar's voice.

"How very thoughtful. Please, thank Lord Falcon for us." Nemo couldn't believe it. "What would Brittany think about this," he wondered, foolishly.

"It is our custom," stammered Nemo, loudly, "to bathe alone" His voice trailed off in embarrassment.

The girls each took a step back. A look of shocked surprise crossed their faces.

"That is our custom as well," said Leah looking from Quasar to Nemo and back again. "If you would just tell us where you would like these things," she continued, slightly confused, "we will leave and you can take your bath."

Quasar smiled broadly. Nemo blushed. His forehead was beaded with sweat.

"Oh," was all Nemo could manage to say. Just then the tent flap opened and an older, heavyset women peered inside.

"What is taking you girls so long?" she asked in mock severity.

Her smile revealed a wide gap between her two front teeth. She wore many golden chains and had double double chins.

"Please, put the baskets right there," said Quasar as he pointed to a little wooden table near the tubs.

Quasar quickly laced up his open shirt. The

older woman held the tent flap high, allowing sunlight to flood the tent. The girls left the baskets as directed, bowed and departed. The woman nodded respectfully, and gently lowered the flap.

Quasar and Nemo were silent as they heard the sound of jingling chains and tinkling bells fade in the distance. They also thought they heard giggles. Quasar could barely look at Nemo without laughing. Nemo simply shrugged his shoulders.

"I thought they were going to..." began Nemo.

"I know what you thought," interrupted Quasar shaking his head. "Take your bath."

Without any more protests Nemo undressed quickly and submerged himself in his tub. Quasar did likewise. It took but a few moments for them to become accustomed to the hot water, which loosened their tense muscles and calmed their nerves. Lightly scented steam swirled around their heads. Never before had Quasar and Nemo felt so relaxed and clean. Never before had they thought that clean could feel so good.

They talked of the ride, the soldiers, the camp, the girls. Slowly, their words grew heavy.

Soon they both fell asleep in the tubs with their heads propped up to one side.

Suddenly, Nemo slipped under the water. He surfaced sputtering loudly and splashed water all over one side of the tent. Quasar awoke with a start.

"What time is it?" he asked Nemo, who still wasn't sure where he was or why he was drowning.

"How should I know?" answered Nemo, sleepily.

Quasar jumped from the tub, wrapped a towel around himself and peeked outside.

"Oh, no. We slept too long. The sun has almost set! Hurry and get dressed, we can't be late!"

Quasar threw a huge towel to Nemo. As they hurried to dress Quasar thought of the Lord Hiram and what was to come.

"Please," begged Quasar. "Please, let me do the talking."

"You forget yourself," said Nemo as he dried his hair. "I alone own Silverglade."

"We are not trying to sell Silverglade. We are trying to save our lives," said Quasar, drying his feet and trying hard not to shout at the new Lord Nemo.

"Brother," he continued, trying to calm himself. "As Counsel to Nemo, Lord of Silverglade, it is only fitting that I would represent you." Quasar glanced at Nemo as he dressed. He seemed to be listening.

"Let us agree," suggested Quasar, "that you will speak to me, privately and I will speak to the Lord Hiram for you."

"Fine," said Nemo, grudgingly.

He stood admiring his clothes, for a moment. He was wearing a dark green shirt with silver embroidery and soft leather pants. It occurred to him that the silver was real.

Quasar was tying his boots when he heard someone cough outside the tent. Nemo was trying on another silk shirt, his third so far. It had no embroidery. He rubbed the soft cloth against his skin.

"That one will have to do, Lord Nemo," said Quasar in a hoarse whisper. "I believe Lord Falcon has come to take us to his father."

Quasar's pants and boots were soft black leather. He was wearing a white silk shirt and a vest made of red tooled leather. He tossed a similar vest to Nemo.

"Just put this on, please." said Quasar.

Nemo was slipping it on over his shirt when Quasar pulled the tent flap open. There stood Lord Falcon.

"I trust my servants took care of you," he said with a smile.

"Yes," replied Quasar. "They brought us more than we could have asked for."

Nemo looked at Lord Falcon and nodded. He couldn't help wondering if the girls had told him everything that had happened.

"Come," said Lord Falcon simply. "The Lord Hiram must not be kept waiting. You must understand certain things," he continued as they walked toward the huge tent. "It is our custom to honor my father. It is the right of the Lord Hiram to speak first, to eat first, to stand first, and to sit first. The meal will not begin for the rest of us until my father begins to eat." Lord Falcon was casual, but clear.

The three approached the huge tent. Nothing they had seen that day, or in fact in their lives, prepared them for the splendor of the main pavilion. It was made of bright white material that seemed as strong as it was beautiful. Gold thread woven into its fabric caused the pavilion to shimmer even in the dim light of dusk. Embroidered golden cords danced on its folds. Large torches ringed the pavilion. Their light reflected all the way to where the golden flag flew; high as a tall tree. Two guards stood at each torch. Quasar noticed that additional guards were positioned discreetly in the shadows.

As they got closer to the tent Quasar and Nemo felt the ground under their feet change. It made a quiet crunching noise as they walked. Unconsciously, they glanced at their feet and were surprised to find that they were now walking on something hard and white.

"We are walking on my father's enemies." said Lord Falcon who had noticed their curiosity.

Quasar looked to his right and left. All around the tent was a three-inch thick layer of hard white granules. Quasar shuddered as he thought of the shattered bones of those defeated in battle.

"What?" said Nemo, who could not control his surprise.

"We are walking on crushed oyster shells,

symbolic of my father's defeated enemies," said Lord Falcon.

Nemo closed his eyes in relief. Quasar breathed deeply.

"All who stand against the Lord Hiram will fall beneath our boots," recited Lord Falcon. "It is a saying," he said with a bright smile. "A true saying," he added.

Lord Falcon paused for a moment before approaching the entrance to the tent. Four guards, stationed at the entrance, stood tall and stiff at attention.

"Remember," said Lord Falcon, quietly. "Sit after he sits. If he is sitting do not stand. Speak only after he has spoken to you. It is our way."

With these instructions in mind Quasar and Nemo followed Lord Falcon into the pavilion, and may as well have entered another world.

Colors, scents, textures and sounds invaded their senses, filling them to capacity. The floor on which they walked was softer than Quasar's bed. Lamps hung high in the tent. Light reflected brightly off the white ceiling. It was as bright inside as noon on the summer solstice. The inner side walls, Quasar noticed, were not white, but were hung with beautiful tapestries. Lord Falcon paused for a moment, nodding to the tapestries.

"These tell the history of my family. Perhaps later I will have time to show them to you." He spoke with quiet respect.

Moving further into the pavilion, Lord Falcon led them through a veiled partition. It shimmered and glistened as they brushed past.

"Those are jewels!" whispered Nemo.

Quasar shushed him with a glance. Guards snapped to attention as Lord Falcon emerged from the veil.

This room was larger than the first one. Servants padded to and fro performing tasks and errands. They nodded politely to Lord Falcon and continued their work. One lit new candles. Another tended to a firebox which radiated warmth but gave off no smoke or flame.

Quasar breathed deeply. Never before had he smelled anything so clean and sweet. Though he didn't know it, a special mild incense made of spices and citrus oil burned in orbs overhead.

Lord Falcon moved still further into the pavilion. They followed him in silence. Quasar glanced at Nemo. He was wide-eyed and ashen.

They walked through several more curtained sections of the tent. Each section was deeper within the tent and each more lavish than the one before. All were manned with servants and armed guards.

"I have never even dreamed of anything like this," said Nemo glancing at Quasar.

At that very moment, Lord Falcon stopped walking. Unfortunately, Nemo did not. He almost tumbled into his unsuspecting host. Lord Falcon did not seem to notice. If he did notice, he pretended not to.

They stood before a thick dark veil decorated by metal shields. Each was a different color. There were ten in all, one for each of the sons of the House of Hiram. Each shield was etched with the now familiar emblem of the twin black hawks. Servants knelt at their feet and helped them remove their boots. Nemo reached out and steadied himself against a black wooden pillar. Its surface was hard and smooth as marble. The servants departed quietly with their boots. No sound could be heard but the faint hiss of burning oil lamps.

Lord Falcon straightened his uniform,

stood erect and nodded to a guard. Quasar swallowed hard, Nemo took a deep breath, and the veil was drawn aside. Silently, they were admitted into the inner chamber of the tent. Finally, they stood before the Lord Hiram.

Ten huge sheets of silk hung from the edges of the round room. They were colored in the same colors as the ten shields and the ten large tents outside. Quasar was beginning to understand the pattern. In the center of the room was a huge round table made of an extraordinary white wood. It was inlaid at the center with a shield of pure gold that was etched with the image of twin black hawks. Lord Falcon took his place at the table. Directly behind him hung a blood-red banner. His nine brothers likewise stood around the table in order of rank, each with his own colored banner for a backdrop.

At the far end of the room, opposite the place they had entered, stood the Lord Hiram. He was tall, broad-shouldered and powerfully built. His silver hair hung almost to his shoulders. He smiled warmly when he saw his guests, but his eyes remained cold steel blue.

On either side of the Lord Hiram was an

empty chair, straight-backed and tall like all the others. Somewhere in another room, musicians started playing softly. A servant moved to usher Quasar and Nemo to their places at the table. Quasar and Nemo found themselves standing at the table with the Lord Hiram between them. To Quasar's right stood Lord Falcon. To Nemo's left there stood the youngest member of the House of Hiram. Unlike his brothers who were uniformed in one color, he was dressed in a multi-colored tunic and a striped cloak.

The table was filled with every manner of food and drink, yet servants continued to bring platters of steaming fare. There was meat, fish, and fowl. Bowls of cooked vegetables and roots were presented. Bread and fruit abounded. Nemo felt a strong urge to eat a grape from a tray set before him. He resisted it.

Closing his eyes and lifting an arm straight up the Lord Hiram offered thanks for his food, his sons and his guests. The simplicity and sincerity of this act surprised Quasar and Nemo more than anything they had seen so far. The words of this prayer were the only words spoken during dinner.

After praying, the Lord Hiram sat and began to eat. Quasar, Nemo and the ten sons of the Lord Hiram sat in unison and ate without speaking. Servants silently attended to every need. Goblets were filled before they were half empty. Trays were presented, removed, refreshed and presented anew. Quasar and Nemo had never seen, much less tasted, most of these foods.

Nemo was just about to reach for another sweet-cake when, without warning, the Lord Hiram stood. The musicians stopped playing. The ten sons stood. Quasar and Nemo followed.

"Falcon, you have done well," said the Lord Hiram in a deep resonant voice. "Thank you for bringing our guests."

Quasar thought the Lord Hiram seemed sincere.

"You're welcome, Father," answered his son.

"I would speak to them, alone. Good night," said the Lord Hiram.

With that, the servants quickly cleared the table and left. Each of his sons embraced the Lord Hiram and departed. With a slight nod he even dismissed his personal guard. They immediately left, seeming to disappear into a veil. Quasar and Nemo were left standing utterly alone with the Lord Hiram himself. He was the biggest man they had ever seen. His hands were huge; double those of the village blacksmith. His fingers thick and callused. No wealthy softness here. With forearms the size of small tree trunks, this man was power incarnate. Looking at his clean-shaven handsome face, Quasar noted that Lord Hiram had passed his chiseled cleft chin to Falcon.

Never before had Quasar seen such strength and such control. "This is true greatness," he thought.

Nemo, on the other hand, could think of nothing. His brain had stopped working when the Lord Hiram fixed his gaze upon him. Nemo felt as if this man could read his very soul.

"My friend, Nemo, Lord of Silverglade," said the Lord Hiram, finally. "How good it is to see you again." His smile was broad and pleasant, his teeth perfectly white.

Nothing in this greeting betrayed sarcasm or double meaning. "Could he really be glad to see Nemo again?" thought Quasar. "Or, is he only pleased that Silverglade is now within his grasp?"

Quasar's self-talk abruptly came to an end as he heard his own name.

"And, Lord Quasar," said the Lord Hiram warmly. "It is good to meet a friend of my friend."

At this, he extended his massive hand to Quasar. His grip bordered on being painful. "In his youth," thought Quasar, "this man must have been unbeatable. Even now, few could best him in a test of strength."

"Thank you, my lord," answered Quasar with a smile as warm as he could manage. As Lord Hiram released his hand Quasar unconsciously wiggled his fingers in relief.

"Lord Nemo and Lord Quasar, I have a request of you," said the Lord Hiram, walking nonchalantly around the table. Nothing in his tone warned the boys of what was to come.

Nemo was silent.

"At least he has remembered to let me do the talking," thought Quasar.

In reality, Nemo could not have spoken to save their lives. "You have only to ask, my Lord," answered Quasar, following him around the table with his eyes, not daring to sit or move.

"Let us drop these titles and pretenses. I shall call you simply Nemo and Quasar."

Nemo paled at these words. The room began to spin.

"This man gets right to the point," said Quasar to himself. "I hope this is the only point we see tonight." He could not help but notice the huge broadsword hanging behind where Lord Hiram now stood. Light seemed to race along its double edge. No mere decoration, this.

"Nemo," continued Lord Hiram. "You were kind enough to entertain me at your home. Now, finally, I have been able to repay that debt."

Nemo stared in silence, listening, waiting.

"While I was there," continued Hiram, "I had one thing in mind. I wanted Silverglade. I offered you more than I have every offered anyone for anything. But you refused me."

Quasar shuddered as the Lord Hiram's eyes hardened. He spoke slowly, deliberately. Turning his back to them, he continued. "I don't mind telling you that made me angry." As he spoke he traced the edge of the sword with his finger.

"But as I rode back to my camp the beauty of Silverglade ministered to my spirit."

He faced them again, smiling.

"We stopped and spent the night in an open glade. I was returned, in my mind, to a simpler time of life. It was a time in my youth when I lived more as you do; an unencumbered time." The Lord Hirm paused. He was, for a moment, lost in thought.

"My father wisely sent me to live and learn about life away from court and glory. Away from all this." The Lord Hiram fingered a heavy gold chain that hung around his neck.

"I do not question the calling God has given me, but I learned much in those uncomplicated days. What I am today is built upon the foundation of that learning." Hiram looked at Quasar and Nemo and breathed deeply. He spoke with unadorned candor.

"I'm afraid, however, that by the time I visited you I had forgotten some of the most important lessons. At that time, wealth had darkened my mind and power corrupted my heart. It happened so slowly. I began to believe what the wags and minstrels say about me."

Hiram looked directly at Nemo and said, "You rescued me."

All was silent within the tent. The air was still. A mild exotic scent flowed around the table as the Lord Hiram moved. He gazed intently at Nemo, then continued. "I had fully intended to kill you if you refused my offer." His voice was low and even. Quasar breathed in deeply. Nemo's breath stopped short. They both stared at their dangerous host.

"I know you knew nothing about all this," continued Lord Hiram, softly. "You simply shared your hospitality with me and refused to be bought. Somehow it was used to set me straight. By losing Silverglade I gained my soul." Hiram's voice was strong and low.

"I stayed several days in a clearing. My time in Silverglade renewed my spirit and helped return my balance. So you see," continued Hiram, "I owe you a great debt."

Nemo took a long deep breath. The color returned to his face. Quasar shifted his weight from one foot to the other.

"Thank you, my Lord," they said in unison.

"Hiram," he corrected, "Please, call me Hiram. In private, let us be simple friends." He motioned them to sit.

And so the night began as neither Quasar nor Nemo could have imagined it. Cautiously, Quasar began dropping hints about the missing sheep and about Silverglade. It soon became apparent, however, that Hiram had lost interest in Silverglade.

"I still love Silverglade, but not the same as before," said Hiram, thoughtfully. "At first, I wanted it as a wedding gift for Casandra, my only daughter." A smile graced his face at the mention of her name. Light sparkled in his eyes.

"Ten wonderful sons have I, each worthy of the kingdom. But, there is only one princess in the House of Hiram. She was to wed Prince Aalon, heir to the throne of Luminus. I had had dealings with his father." Hiram looked deeply into some distant memory. A darkness seemed to eclipse his face and then the light returned.

"It was, at first, a political arrangement," he continued quietly. "However, God smiled on us. As they both grew older, they grew together. When their love began to expand into passion, it became time for them to marry."

Hiram paused and stared into the shadows of the tent. Quasar noticed his eyes glistened with a far-away look. Quasar and Nemo exchanged glances.

"Though I was sure Casandra would be happy," he continued, "I could not tolerate the thought of never seeing her again. And so I made my plans." Hiram leaned in closer to them. He smiled and looked at Nemo.

"Silverglade is mid-way between our two kingdoms. It is a long journey overland, but by sea, it is a brief voyage from either kingdom. The region is stable and safe. Silverglade is far enough from the coast to be secure from naval attack, yet close enough to the port of Mecenas to be convenient to our ships." He paused waiting for some sign of understanding. Receiving none from either boy, he sighed lightly, and continued.

"I had hoped that Silverglade would serve as a halfway point between our kingdoms." He spoke now like a patient tutor.

"I wanted to create a retreat where both our families could meet away from court and duty. My dear wife, Queen Elisa, would also enjoy a time away from the throne. I am afraid in my absence, she must perform many duties."

Hiram grew quiet and remained so for such

a long time that both Quasar and Nemo wondered what to do. Quasar looked around. No sign of servant or guard could be seen. Almost nothing could be heard, but the deep slow breathing of their host.

Quasar noticed an oil lamp, one of a dozen or more burning high above them. It sputtered and went out. He shrugged his shoulders at Nemo's unvoiced question. Nemo played with a crumb on the table, flicking it between his fingers. Not knowing what to do, Nemo almost stood to leave. He was startled when Hiram suddenly clapped his hands loudly. In an instant two servants and three guards appeared.

"Bring refreshments for my guests, please," commanded Hiram. The servants bowed and the guards retreated. Hiram still didn't speak until after the servants delivered a tray of hot tea and sweet cakes. He broke a small, warm, sweet cake in half and dipped it into a sauce made from berries and cream. Taking a sip of the strong aromatic tea he sighed deeply and continued.

"I am afraid the wedding gift is no longer needed. Prince Aalon has been killed by assassins. Even now, his father, King Triiton, battles traitors for his throne."

As he spoke, his voice became dangerously even in tone as if all emotions were held in check and focused on one thought.

"I have promised my support. That is why I am here with my army. This camp will serve as the launching place for our attack. I hope they won't be needed, but we can summon additional troops in a matter of days."

In truth, the troops on the island could arrive in just a few hours, depending on the tide and the winds. Few knew this secret.

"I will be pleased to avenge Prince Aalon's death," announced Hiram loudly.

The sweet-cake crumbled between his thumb and forefinger. A shiver ran down Quasar's back as Hiram's hard blue steel eyes again narrowed.

I never want to have this man as an enemy, thought Quasar.

"Preparations are almost complete," said Hiram coldly. "When all information is gathered, when everything is ready, the sons of the House of Hiram will be sent into battle. My youngest three sons, Vine, Reed and Gannon, will be tested for the first time. Falcon will lead the campaign," he said proudly. Then Hiram again grew silent.

After listening to the problems of King Triiton and the Lord Hiram, Quasar and Nemo felt their own problems shrink in significance. There was still the question of missing sheep, but it had been foolish to think that the Lord Hiram was a thief. Whatever evil threatened Quasar and Nemo, they could not believe it was from this man.

"Perhaps when this is over my sons and I could visit Silverglade again?" asked Hiram wistfully. "It might be a necessary sojourn on our way home from war."

The tone of his voice was suddenly dark and ominous. Nemo seized the opportunity.

"Yes, by all means," he said enthusiastically. "Please, let me extend an open invitation. The House of Hiram is welcome in Silverglade, anytime."

This was the most Nemo had spoken the whole evening, and, as it happened, it was almost the last thing spoken at all.

"I have enjoyed our little talk," said Hiram wearily.

Without further comment he stood. Quasar and Nemo followed his lead. He smiled and embraced them both as they had seen him embrace his own sons. Quasar was surprised by this show of affection. Nemo felt suddenly trapped by the man's strength. It was like being in the grasp of a huge, gentle bear.

Hiram clapped again. Servants returned with their boots and a guard, dressed all in white, appeared silently.

"Good night, my friends," said The Lord Hiram. "The guard will escort you to your quarters." With that, the audience ended.

The guard led the boys out of the pavilion and into the night air. No one spoke. The camp was quiet. After so long in the brightness and warmth of the pavilion, the darkness and chill of night came as a hard reality to the boys. Finally, the guard brought them to a tent. It was not the same tent in which they had bathed. Comfortable beds, night garments and clothing for the morning awaited them. A small, ornate brazier full of glowing embers provided heat and a little light.

"Did you ever expect anything like this in all of your life?" whispered Nemo. His tongue had loosened and he was eager to talk.

"No," said Quasar, quietly.

"Just think," said Nemo excitedly. "When the day started we were only shepherds, trying to protect our flocks. Now, by some strange turn of events, we are friends of the Lord Hiram! One of the most powerful men on earth. Perhaps the most powerful man on earth."

"We are still 'only shepherds'," said Quasar sharply. "And our sheep are still in danger. As for the Lord Hiram, he has indeed been friendly. He has been kinder than I thought possible. But after tomorrow, we may never see him again. If we ever stood in his way, he would kill us in a heartbeat."

"I think you are wrong," responded Nemo, defensively.

"Keep you voice down," warned Quasar.

"Even if we never see him again," continued Nemo quietly, "This is the most exciting thing that has ever happened to me, and you, too."

"We have been fortunate," said Quasar sleepily. "Can't we just go to sleep?"

Nemo's irritation with Quasar faded. "We have much to be thankful for," he said calmly. "Goodnight, Quasar."

"Goodnight, brother," answered Quasar.

They both prayed and thanked God for the Lord Hiram. Neither they nor he would have dreamed how the tapestry of their lives was being woven together.

CHAPTER 4
Colors

$\mathcal{T}$he next day dawned bright and clear. Quasar and Nemo awoke later than usual. Never before had they slept in such comfort. They hurriedly dressed in the clothes that had been provided for them. Both had been given soft black leather pants, as before. They each had a simple white undershirt, and a black overgarment, like a jacket, made of light wool. The clothes fit perfectly. They wore the same boots as the previous night. When they had dressed, Nemo opened the tent flap and almost tripped over his breakfast.

"Quasar, look here," he said happily.

In his hands he held a large basket of fruit and bread. At his feet was a tray holding two mugs and two ceramic pots. One pot was full of hot tea and the other contained a frothy hot drink that was unknown to them. It was dark, thick, creamy and sweet. Quasar and Nemo attacked breakfast zealously.

"You look good in a mustache," laughed Quasar.

The sweet drink had left a dark brown stain across Nemo's upper lip. It matched his curly brown hair. Nemo wiped it off and smiled good naturedly. Quasar looked askance at his friend. He had never seen Nemo smile first thing in the morning.

Lord Falcon entered the tent just as they were finishing breakfast. He was again dressed in a red uniform and cape. Accompanying him was a thin young man dressed in a multi-colored tunic and a striped cloak. It was the same young man who had sat to Nemo's left at dinner. Quasar and Nemo quickly stood.

"Lords Quasar and Nemo, I would like to introduce my youngest brother, Lord Gannon." Gannon had thick golden hair, like Quasar's, only longer. His eyes were a brilliant green. He was slightly shorter than both Quasar and Nemo and looked very much like Falcon. He had the same intense look and the same cleft in his chiseled chin.

Gannon shook hands with Nemo and smiled. He locked eyes with Quasar as they shook hands. *Does everyone in this family have a steel grip?* thought Quasar.

"We thought you might like a tour of the camp," continued Falcon.

"Oh, yes," answered Nemo as he put down his mug.

"That would be excellent!" added Quasar excitedly.

He followed Nemo and the others out of the tent. Quasar hurried to catch up with Falcon while Gannon stayed back a moment with Nemo.

"I, too, want to grow a mustache," said Gannon with a kind smile, "But I think you'll have to wait with me a little while longer."

Nemo's hand quickly rubbed the brown liquid from his lip.

"I think I'd better avoid that drink," laughed Nemo. "Thank you."

Falcon and Gannon escorted the boys around camp. Quasar and Nemo were amazed to learn that life in camp was filled with work, drills, preparation and practice. They had imagined a life filled with acts of glory and honor, not tedium and training. This tour was as much a break for Falcon and Gannon as it was a treat for Quasar and Nemo. Falcon happily watched as his young brother took over leading the tour; answering questions, pointing, explaining. Falcon stayed back of the three, watching, smiling, as they began walking through camp.

"The Greens report to my brother, Reed," explained Gannon as he pointed to the area just past his own striped tents.

Quasar and Nemo looked and saw dozens of lesser green tents pitched around Lord Reed's large forest green tent. The tents were not being used as barracks, but as a communal workplace.

"Reed is almost two years older than I," said Gannon. There was a slight hesitation in his voice.

He looked carefully for a moment at his two new friends, unsure of himself.

"It was his men who first met you on the road," he said, finally.

Quasar and Nemo were amazed at all the activity around them. In The Greens, at that moment, a number of men were weaving branches and grasses onto dark netting. Others were taking finished netting and covering themselves with it. These were sentries about to go on duty. Their green uniforms, soot-smeared faces and camouflage netting would render them invisible in the forest. Soon, the men whom they replaced would return with their nets, leave them to be repaired or refreshed, and then get some food and rest. Life in camp was an intricate dance of well-ordered cycles.

Gannon led the group toward a set of wine-colored tents where a cloud of delicious aromas welcomed them. As they left the Green area a green-clad soldier quietly set down his netting and carefully followed them.

"This is my brother Vine's area," said Gannon as he walked the outskirts of the wine colored tents. "He is the third youngest of my father's sons."

Quasar and Nemo were astonished by the vast amount of food being prepared in *Vine's Wines*, as Gannon called it.

"Maybe we can return here closer to lunch time," said Gannon smiling impishly. Falcon laughed, reading his little brother's mind.

"Gannon is forever snatching fruit, fresh baked rolls and sweet cakes from Vine's storehouse." Falcon explained, smiling warmly at his little brother. Gannon laughed.

Often with young men there develops competition which can end in meanness, or worse, bloodshed. It is a blessing, thought Falcon, that my brother and these two have nothing to prove to one another. They seem like longtime friends.

Suddenly, Falcon's thoughts were interrupted by his brother's voice.

"How can that be!" shouted Gannon excitedly. "You are trying to deceive me!"

"No, it is true. Really!" shouted Nemo in return.

Falcon quickly looked from one boy to the other.

"You and I really were born on the same day," continued Nemo. "We could be twins!"

Falcon took a deep breath. For a moment he had feared a quarrel.

"And I was born five months and one year before you." laughed Quasar.

With this revelation, the three boys linked arms and paraded through camp, talking, laughing. Quasar noticed that everywhere they went soldiers snapped to attention.

Falcon walked a little behind the threesome,

arms clasped behind his back. He was surprised to see his brother so animated. Gannon was sometimes troubled in spirit. Falcon loved his young brother, almost as a son. He was pleased to see the effect these two had on him. Nemo, especially, brought out the best in Gannon. Falcon thought of the future and sighed heavily.

I wish Gannon could go back with them to Silverglade instead of going to war, he thought to himself. He could not shake a growing dread that this campaign would not end well.

Leaving *Vine's Wines*, Gannon led the tour past the deep purple enclave of Lord Ram and the dark blue area of Lord Norrom.

"I wish we could take you to Ram's other place," said Gannon with admiration. "Here he only has the designers who plan and draw. Outside of camp is where the real fun takes place."

"Brother," said Falcon kindly, "Lord Nemo and Lord Quasar rode through Ram's outer camp with me on their way here."

"Was that what we passed on the hill?" asked Nemo in wonder. "The place where all those big things were being built?"

"Yes," said Falcon without expression. His

voice was flat and quiet. "Ram makes machines for battle."

"Did you see the one that throws huge rocks?" interrupted Gannon. "It can also throw barrels of burning oil and other things!" Gannon's eyes flashed with visions of towers, ramps and machines of war. "Ram can make anything," he said excitedly.

To Gannon, war was still a glorious adventure. Falcon smiled sadly at his brother, the man-child. He remembered his own youthful fantasies and how harshly they had been dispelled.

Quasar and Nemo passed Norrom's area. Compared with the others, this one seemed tame. There were a number of parked wagons and a good many crates, but very little activity.

"Lord Norrom is in charge of transport," said Gannon. "But he does a lot more than it looks."

"Norrom is in charge of the navy," added Falcon with a smile, "but my little brother, here, doesn't like the sea. His stomach would prefer that he stay on land."

Gannon seemed not to hear his brother's tease.

"Oh, look" exclaimed Gannon as they walked on. "They're sending messages."

Gannon pointed to an area of sky blue tents. A cloud of pigeons erupted heavenward.

"This is Herald's place," added Falcon.

Quasar and Nemo were astonished by this area. One part was dedicated to pigeons, with rows upon rows of cages housing hundreds, perhaps thousands of birds. The cages were marked with words written in large letters; presumably, the names of distant cities to which the homing pigeons would fly. Several boys, younger than Gannon, were caring for the birds. A man approached and spoke to one of the boys. He ran off, but almost instantly returned with a bird. The man gently stroked the pigeon's head and neck. Then, after calming the bird, he attached a small metal cylinder to its leg. When all was ready, the man threw the bird into the air. It made one small circle around the camp, and another larger circle, then it was gone.

"Where is that bird going?" asked Nemo of no one in particular. The man turned, walked several steps closer, and looked to Lord Falcon. Falcon nodded slightly.

"It's taking a message to a nearby island, sir. My Lord Herald has had birds there for several years now. They always go back to where they were born."

Quasar would like to have learned more about these birds, but the tour would not wait. Close by, men polished boots, saddles, and curved golden horns. Everything here was orderly and spotless. Horses stood waiting, fully saddled. Several uniformed riders also waited nearby. Quasar thought he recognized the man with the horn who had ridden with Falcon when they first met. But as they passed, the man would not acknowledge him. He just stood at attention, like the others, and stared straight ahead.

Nearby, a group of men stood, some with small flags on short rods and others with brightly polished metal disks. The men with the flags waved them in sequence, then stopped and watched as another group waved back in answer. The men holding the disks made them flash in the sunlight. Those flashes were answered by other flashes of light from a distant ridge.

Quasar and Nemo stopped and stared, transfixed by the colored flags and flashes of light.

"What?" was all Nemo could manage.

"They are talking to one another," explained Gannon. "Herald helps us communicate with outposts far from camp. He has horses and riders that can travel for hours, and runners who can go where horses cannot. The flags and disks are usually used in battle. They can send commands and information all over the battlefield." Gannon's excitement revealed an open love and respect for his brother Herald.

"He also informs the camp of daily events like meals and the changing of the guard," added Falcon. "His drummers signal troop movements. His hornsmen announce visitors or even warn of an attack. Herald has been very clever in all that he has designed. He helps everything move smoothly."

It was obvious that Falcon too, respected and loved Herald.

As if on cue, a crisp flurry resounded from the nearest hilltop. All eyes momentarily turned toward the sound. A lone rider was descending the same path Quasar and Nemo had ridden the day before. Apparently the signal was of no consequence, for all work resumed as quickly as it had ceased.

"It is nothing," said Gannon looking back at Quasar and Nemo. "Come. Let me show you Falcon's troops."

Gannon was thrilled with the opportunity to honor his eldest brother. Falcon seemed less than excited. As they walked to Falcon's area, a lone soldier, dressed in green, kept them in sight. He carefully walked behind tents and in shadows so as to not be seen by anyone on the tour. To the casual eye, he would seem occupied by some unrelated task, but he always kept the four in view.

"There is really nothing to see here," said Falcon as they entered the Red area. "We are just soldiers."

"My brother is too modest," chided Gannon. "Falcon's men are the best of the best. They train the hardest; fight the hardest. They have never known defeat, never. His color is red because they shed their blood more than any of the others. It is a great honor to be selected to join The Talons," said Gannon reverently.

"The Talons?" asked Quasar and Nemo in unison.

"That's what I call 'em," Gannon smiled.

"Everyone else just calls 'em 'The Reds'," he added.

Gannon paused, giving Falcon the opportunity to add to the description of The Reds. When he did not speak, Gannon continued.

"To become one of The Reds is the greatest honor any soldier can hope for." Gannon looked again to his brother for comment, but Falcon was silent.

"They must first distinguish themselves in their own division, and be recommended by one of my brothers," continued Gannon proudly. "That's the easy part."

"My men work hard," admitted Falcon reluctantly. "I am proud of them." After an awkward silence he added. "Come, let us see Tulmar's work."

Falcon led the group away from his own red tents toward the fire orange tents of his father's second son.

This area was different than all the others. In addition to tents there were also buildings, made of sod, wood and stone. The air was heavy with the smoke of many fires. The pulsing sound of huge bellows and the resonating ring of metal against metal vibrated the very ground they walked on.

"My brother has perfected the art of metallurgy," shouted Gannon over the noise.

They walked past several huts in which blacksmiths toiled. Their eyes stung from the smoke of many fires. The roar of bellows and the ring of hammer against anvil was deafening.

"He even left our land to study under foreign masters," said Gannon loudly. "When he returned, he had grown in body and in mind," he added. Clearly he was in awe of his older brother.

A hiss of steam and the sound of water drew their attention to a nearby shack.

"Yes. Yes! That's it. That is it!" came a loud thundering voice.

Out from behind a veil of smoke and steam stepped a huge twin of the Lord Hiram, only younger. Quasar and Nemo again marveled that any man could be so strong. He stood half a head taller than Falcon, who was himself taller than most men. His arms were the size of small trees and his chest exploded from behind a black leather apron. Sweat oozed from his body. His hair was short and might have been blond, but one couldn't see for sure. Soot covered his hair as it did the rest of him.

"Ah, brother Tulmar," shouted Falcon in surprise. "We were just talking about you. I'm sure you remember..."

"Falcon," interrupted Tulmar excitedly. "Just look at this, Falcon." Tulmar lifted a shinning sliver sword. "I've done it, Falcon. At last, I've done it!"

Tulmar still had not acknowledged Quasar, Nemo or his brother Gannon.

"This blade can be sharpened to a finer edge and more easily than anything else we have. And, it will keep its edge longer, too."

Tulmar paused for a moment and glanced at Gannon.

"Little brother," he said in genuine surprise. A broad smile covered his sweaty face. "Just look here! This sword is lighter and stronger than any other on earth." He sliced the sword through the air, then suddenly tossed it, handle first, to Gannon.

Pleased with himself that he caught it, Gannon joined in his brother's excitement.

"What new metal is this, Tulmar?" asked

Gannon in wonder.

He gently ran his finger down the razored edge of the blade. Falcon, Quasar and Nemo crowded near to see and touch the thing.

"It is not a new metal. It is forged with a new technique." answered Tulmar. "It is all very simple."

He took a deep breath as if to begin a long and complicated explanation, but stopped short. Fixing his gaze on Quasar and Nemo, he quickly snatched back the sword.

"Ah, our guests from last night," he said with a frozen smile. "How good it is to see you again."

Tulmar wiped the sweat from his eyes. Looking down at the sword and then back up he added slowly, "It is nothing, really."

"I'll tell you all about it when I have more time." Tulmar paused, struggling for words. "Just look at me," he said opening his arms wide to reveal the dirt from this morning's labors. "I have to go clean up for lunch."

With that, Lord Tulmar bowed slightly and disappeared back into the smoky steam from which he had appeared, taking the mysterious sword with him.

"My brother is right," said Falcon, leading the group out of the smoke and noise toward a bright yellow compound. "We must hurry if we are to see the rest of the camp before lunch."

Following his older brother's lead Gannon added, "Let's see if Shank is working his archers."

Gannon ran ahead through a group of yellow tents to where a shooting range had been built. Being the youngest, Gannon was never able to beat any of his brothers in contests of strength. But when it came to archery he was, more or less, on common ground.

Shank had taken a special interest in Gannon, and spent hours patiently instructing him in archery. That diligence had been a good investment. Now, it was said within the House of Hiram that Gannon was second in accuracy only to Shank himself. Several of his brothers could still best him in distance, but Gannon was sure, as his strength increased with age, he would surpass them all.

Falcon, Quasar and Nemo caught up with Gannon near a row of longbowmen who were receiving instruction. Three tall men walked up and down the line, making comments to and correcting the archers. The tallest of the three wore a uniform and cape just like Falcon's, except that it was bright yellow.

"Look at him," whispered Nemo. "That must be Lord Shank. His eyes, his face, his hair, the way he stands. He looks exactly like Falcon, only younger."

Lord Shank slapped Gannon on the back. "Little brother!" exclaimed Shank with genuine surprise. "I am so glad to see you. I could use your help right now."

"And Falcon," added Shank as Falcon walked up. "What brings you here?" Shank did not yet recognize Quasar and Nemo.

"I was hoping we could show our guests some archery," said Gannon, not waiting for Falcon to answer the question.

Falcon forgave his brother's zeal. He knew Gannon wanted to impress his two new friends.

"Excellent," said Shank, taking Gannon by the arm. "I was just trying to instruct these Greens. Reed asked that these men learn the longbow."

Shank motioned to the line of men

standing nearby. "These fine men are skilled at the crossbow," said Shank loudly enough for all to hear, "but, as you know, the longbow is different."

A murmer of agreement rippled through the line of men. "Perhaps you would help me in a demonstration?" Shank asked Gannon quietly.

"Anything," answered Gannon smiling. He looked back at Falcon, Quasar and Nemo, eyes sparkling in joyous pride. This was more than he had hoped for.

Handing Gannon a bow and quiver Shank led his brother to stand in front of the line of archers. In one smooth action, Gannon strung the bow. He then selected an arrow. Holding it to his eye, Gannon slowly rotated it between his thumb and index finger, examining the shaft for any curve or defect. Upon the shaft was fastened three feathers; two black and one bright yellow. He gently smoothed them.

"Please note," began Shank, addressing the men, "Lord Gannon will stand with his feet one meter apart; his left foot forward, his left hand holding the bow."

Gannon assumed the proper position as Shank continued.

"His weight is on his right foot. His right hand holds the arrow and string." Gannon fitted arrow to string, making sure the yellow feather pointed away from his body.

"Lord Gannon will now take aim at the target," said Shank with a nod to his brother.

Gannon pointed the arrow skyward and gracefully drew the string to full ready. He then carefully took aim, slowly lowering the arrow into position. All heard the familiar twang of a perfect release.

The arrow flew true, striking a target some 60 paces away. The shot was faultless, hitting a small red heart in the center of the target.

"Well done, brother!" shouted Lord Shank. Gannon smiled to himself. Falcon, Quasar and Nemo joined the line of Greens in enthusiastic cheers for the youngest son of the Lord Hiram.

Gannon walked back to Falcon, Quasar and Nemo, smiling. "Would you like to try a shot?" he asked, handing the bow to Quasar.

"Oh, no thank you," replied Quasar with a polite laugh.

He wasn't afraid of losing; he was afraid of winning. *In a situation like this*, he said to himself, *winning could be the quickest way to losing*.

"I'd like to give it a try," volunteered Nemo, taking the challenge and the bow. "You make it look so easy," he said with a smile.

Quasar looked at his friend and sighed. Nemo was the best archer he knew. He was sure that Nemo could equal Gannon's shot. Quasar wanted to remind Nemo of one simple truth: It is unwise to embarrass the son of a King.

We have nothing to gain by winning, Quasar wanted to whisper. *Why risk making Gannon an enemy?* his inner voice asked. But he could say nothing aloud without the others hearing him. *Nemo wouldn't listen anyway*, he said to himself.

Gannon and Nemo walked to the firing line. Nemo nodded as Gannon spoke. The others could not hear what he said. Gannon stepped back. Nemo selected an arrow and checked it for defects. Holding it in one hand, he selected another and examined it carefully.

"Oh no!" thought Quasar. He had seen Nemo do this before.

Holding one arrow in his bow hand, Nemo

set the other to string and took aim. In a flash of incredible speed, Nemo released the first arrow, then aimed and shot the second. It had taken but a heartbeat. Both shots were flawless.

Falcon, Gannon, and Shank were silent. They looked at each other for a moment, and then back at the target.

"I don't believe it!" shouted Gannon as he ran toward the target.

Falcon and Shank followed at a brisk walk. The Green bowmen all began talking at once. Nemo turned, smiling broadly, and walked back to where Quasar stood alone. Quasar glared at his friend.

"What's wrong with you?" asked Nemo, offended by the look. "That was a great shot, even if you won't say so."

"You had to show off," whispered Quasar hotly.

"You're just sorry you didn't try," responded Nemo, shaking his head at Quasar's response. He had never seen Quasar jealous before.

"What good will it do making Gannon our enemy by embarrassing him?" whispered

Quasar, a little more calmly.

"What?" asked Nemo, slowly. Quasar had gotten his attention.

"The Lord Hiram has been very kind to us. We still don't know why. His sons have reflected that kindness," said Quasar. He took a long breath. "One little mistake could change it all."

As Quasar spoke he looked toward Falcon, Shank and Gannon. The three stood near the target, engaged in an animated conversation. Lord Shank motioned to one of the instructors who ran to him, received orders, and ran back to The Greens.

On command, The Greens reassembled in a line, turned and marched away, followed by the two instructors. Quasar and Nemo were left utterly alone. Hidden by nearby brush the Green shadow, who had been following them, took note of everything.

"I see what you mean," said Nemo, his joy replaced by growing apprehension.

"Lord Quasar, Lord Nemo," shouted Falcon. "If you please," he said motioning them to join him at the target.

Quasar and Nemo waved and began

slowly walking to join the others.

"Hurry up," shouted Gannon wildly. "You walk like condemned men to the gallows."

"I wish he hadn't said that," mumbled Nemo. Quasar nodded, forcing a smile.

As Quasar and Nemo approached, the three stepped apart to reveal the target. Nemo's first arrow had struck the very center of the heart, just left of Gannon's arrow. His second arrow had struck slightly above Gannon's. The three points formed a precise triangle.

"It was just a lucky shot," said Quasar quickly.

"Two lucky shots," added Nemo. "I mean, he's right," Nemo added, looking quickly at Quasar. "It was just a lucky shot," he said correcting himself.

"He couldn't do it again if he tried his hardest," continued Quasar.

"I couldn't do it again if my life depended on it," interjected Nemo. "No!" he said loudly, seeing Quasar flinch. "I mean, I couldn't do it again if I tried my hardest; like he said," Nemo forced a smile, but it just made things worse.

"That was not luck," insisted Falcon.

"Neither I nor my men have ever seen anything like that before," said Lord Shank stepping forward. "Nor have Reed's, I'd wager."

"I'm sorry," said Nemo, looking hopefully from one brother to the next.

"Sorry?" bellowed all three.

"He didn't mean to embarrass you in front of your men," said Quasar in Nemo's defense.

"I didn't mean to embarrass you at all," added Nemo.

"Embarrass?" asked Falcon looking to his two younger brothers.

Shank and Gannon both shook their heads. "We're not embarrassed," they said in unison.

"I'm amazed," laughed Gannon.

"I'd like you to teach me how to get such luck," smiled Shank.

"I'm impressed," said Falcon.

Gannon pulled the arrows from the target and handed them to Nemo. "Come, show us how you do it."

"We insist," said the brothers gently turning Quasar and Nemo around by their shoulders. The five quickly walked back to the firing line.

"Now, you must try again," said Shank.

"Try your hardest, as if your life depended on it," chuckled Gannon.

His two brothers exploded in laughter. Quasar hid his surprise behind a smile. Nemo breathed deeply.

"All right," yielded Nemo. "I'll give it my best shot."

Nemo took up his position and, holding one arrow and the bow in his left hand, set the second arrow to string and took aim.

Again, Nemo released the first arrow and then in a flash, aimed and shot the second. The first arrow struck dead center in the heart. The second arrow split the first. Nemo surprised even himself. Quasar, Falcon, Shank and Gannon erupted in cheers and laughter. Nemo smiled.

Suddenly, the earth began to shake as the thunder of hoofs interrupted the laughter. The five turned to see a hundred lancers riding past, five abreast. From their lances flew the silver banner of Lord Kyler, fourth-born son of the

House of Hiram. Twenty rows of heavily armored lancers rode past, each lowering his lance in a salute to Falcon, Shank and Gannon. The hoofs pounded the ground in unison.

"Come on," shouted Gannon, leaving bow and arrows with Shank. "We're in time to see them practice."

Gannon ran toward the shimmering silver camp of his brother Kyler.

"Your speed and skill would be useful here," said Shank as Nemo turned to follow Gannon.

"It just takes practice," answered Nemo, dismissing his skill. He gave Shank a friendly wave, then ran to catch up with Gannon.

Falcon and Quasar bid Shank a hasty good-bye and then also ran to join Gannon. None seemed to notice the Green soldier sitting near a bush, weaving leaves into a net. He did not even look up as they passed.

By the time the four reached the parade grounds, the lancers' drill was almost finished. They were in time, however, to see a practice run of the Grand Charge. Quasar and Nemo watched silently as the horsemen rode, turned and pivoted in formation. Commands were issued by drum cadence and horn.

"The Grand Charge is designed to penetrate the front lines of an entrenched army," explained Falcon. "Once the line is breached, the infantry, coming behind the lancers, pours through the hole." Falcon remarked sadly. "At least, that's the theory."

"To practice, Kyler sets up those bales of hay," said Gannon pointing to the far end of the field, where sheaves stood in a long line. His lightheartedness was in sharp contrast to Falcon's somber tone.

"They represent the battle line of some well armed enemy," said Falcon slowly.

He no longer watched the Lancers, but stared over the distant mountains, as if lost in some far away memory.

"In a real battle, the enemy would first be weakened by a long barrage from Shank's archers," continued Falcon. "The final volley of arrows actually flys over the heads of the charging Lancers. If the horsemen are too fast, they will be killed by our own arrows. If they are too slow, the enemy will have time to recover from the barrage. In the Grand Charge, timing is everything."

Falcon's words were draped in shadows from the past. His tone was so dark that Gannon, Quasar and Nemo all followed his gaze to the mountains. A splash of bright yellow returned their attention to the practice field.

"Look," shouted Gannon. "Shank is bringing some of his men to the drill!"

A column of archers, dressed in yellow battle gear, was running into position behind the line of Lancers.

"This will be exciting!" said Gannon with a broad smile.

"Are they really going to shoot?" asked Nemo, eyes wide in wonder.

Gannon nodded "yes", too wrapped up in events on the field to speak.

"Isn't that a little dangerous?" asked Quasar in disbelief.

"They use practice arrows, tipped with dull clay ends, not sharp metal points," answered Falcon, patiently. "If they strike a rider the worst thing that can happen is a big bruise. The rider will remember the pain. It could save his life one day."

Quasar and Nemo nodded in understanding, and returned their attention to the field. Shank's men were now in position. At his command, the archers aimed and shot as one. The volley flew true, filling the sheaves with arrows.

Suddenly, a horn sounded and a cry arose from the lancers as they spurred their horses to action. The entire line rushed forward. The ground rumbled with the pounding of four hundred galloping hoofs. Again arrows were set to string. Shank's men stood ready. After a long pause another trumpet sounded the command and arrows flew again.

Quasar and Nemo held their breaths, watching the arrows arch toward the line of horsemen. The lancers thundered closer and closer to the straw enemy. Arrows raced overhead.

"They're not going to make it!" shouted Nemo.

"Just watch," answered Gannon, breathlessly.

Suddenly, shouting, "Death from above!"

the riders lowered their lances and leaned forward. Barely clearing the lancers' heads, arrows stormed upon the sheaves. Moments later lances pierced the practice enemy. The horses rode through a cloud of straw. Shaft and hoof did their deadly work. Not one bale was left standing.

A roar of approval rose from the archers. Gannon jumped in the air, yelling. Quasar and Nemo cheered. Falcon turned quietly and walked away, head bowed in thought. Quasar paused and followed him with his eyes. "That soldier has a deep wound," he whispered to himself. Only the Green walking nearby heard him.

A lancer broke ranks and rode to where Falcon walked. Straw covered his long red hair and silver uniform. Lord Kyler reigned in his horse. Snorting and champing, it stopped next to Falcon.

"Did you see it?" asked Kyler. He was out of breath from leading the charge.

"Well done, brother, well done," said Falcon, sincerely. "No one will stand against the lancer's 'Death From Above'."

Kyler nodded. "We shall speak at lunch," he said smiling.

"At lunch, then," answered Falcon, returning the smile. Lord Kyler turned and rode away.

Gannon, Quasar and Nemo ran up moments later. They had wanted to congratulate Kyler, but were too late.

"That was great!" said Gannon as he watched his brother ride away.

The lancers had already assembled and were leaving the grounds in formation. Shank's men were gathering the arrows from the hay.

"Let's get ready for lunch," said Falcon. "If we hurry," he said to Gannon with a wink, "you can show our guests how to steal sweet cakes from brother Vine."

Falcon put his arm around his brother affectionately. In return, Gannon jabbed him in the ribs, then ran laughing toward his own striped tents.

"We haven't seen my men, yet," he shouted back to Falcon. "Race you to my tent," he said, laughing.

Without hesitation, Falcon ran off after

Gannon, leaving behind a surprised Quasar and Nemo.

"Come on," laughed Nemo, joining the race.

Quasar hated being last. Instead of following Nemo, he ran to a signalman who stood with his mount nearby.

"May I borrow your horse?" he asked the startled man. "I need to catch up with Lord Falcon."

The soldier smiled kindly. He knew of the visitors and had seen the start of the foot race.

"Good luck," said the soldier handing Quasar the reins.

"My name is Sage. Please, sir, if possible, return her to me at Lord Herald's compound, when you are done."

"Thank you, Sage," said Quasar, cheerfully. "You'll have her back before lunch," he promised as he rode away.

Quasar could see the striped tents belonging to Gannon in the far distance. He could also see Nemo running a distant third behind Falcon and Gannon. Though Gannon still was in the lead, Falcon was gaining on him quickly. They appeared to be heading for Gannon's main tent. Quasar rode around the outer ring of tents.

"You lose little brother!" Falcon laughed loudly as he passed Gannon.

"Not yet!" answered Gannon redoubling his effort.

Nemo was hopelessly in third place.

"At least I'm ahead of Quasar," panted Nemo, comforting himself.

The three were a dozen paces from Gannon's main tent, Falcon in the lead, when suddenly Quasar strolled out from behind the tent and waved. Falcon was so surprised he tripped, barely keeping on his feet. Gannon kept running, almost passing his brother. Nemo stopped running altogether.

They gathered around Quasar, too breathless to speak. Quasar was not even winded. Falcon leaned forward, hands on his knees. Gannon swayed back and forth trying to catch his breath. Nemo walked up, arms folded in front, shaking his head in disbelief. To make things worse, his side hurt. The one question,

"How", was yet unasked.

With perfect timing the untethered horse wandered out from behind the tent and nudged Quasar's back. The magic was broken. Quasar smiled meekly.

"I try to keep ahead by using my head," he said, gently pushing away the horse. Falcon and Gannon exploded in laughter.

"I hate it when he says that," grumbled Nemo. In reality, no one admired Quasar more than Nemo.

Quasar looked around Gannon's area. It was unlike any of the other compounds. From what he could see, some of the tents were filled with scrolls and maps, others held tables and bottles that were oddly shaped and colored. In some tents men worked with liquids, powders and roots. Bundles of herbs hung from racks, drying in the air. As he looked further, he could see tents in which the sick or injured were being tended by healers. Other tents housed scribes furiously working on scrolls.

Falcon stood and surveyed the grounds.

"As you can see," he began, still a little winded, "the men working here do not wear the uniform of soldiers. They wear the long robes of academia, striped, of course, in Lord Gannon's color. Here are our finest minds; scholars, scientists, physicians."

An old man with a long white beard shuffled past. Never acknowledging Lords Falcon and Gannon, he seemed absorbed in conversation with several beardless young men.

"He is Brohmer, Master of Chemistry," said Gannon. He whispered so as not to disturb the old man's discussion. "They are his apprentices."

"My brother," added Falcon, "has studied with all of the Masters."

"I was just another apprentice," said Gannon humbly.

"Yes, but you started very young, and did very well," boasted Falcon. "Gannon studied astronomy, chemistry, mathematics, Medicinal Arts, and some others," said Falcon, turning to Quasar and Nemo. Falcon was proud of his little brother. "What have I left out, brother?" asked Falcon.

"Nothing that I can remember," said Gannon, untruthfully.

"Cartography!" cried Falcon, laughing.

"That was it. You had to survey the coastline of our kingdom, but you discovered seasickness instead."

Quasar and Nemo couldn't help laughing with Falcon.

"Thank you, brother," said Gannon sarcastically.

In the distance, three blasts of a horn signaled the time.

"We must hurry," said Gannon, "if we are to be on time."

"One thing, please," said Quasar. "I borrowed this horse from one of Lord Herald's men. His name is Sage."

Falcon and Gannon looked at Quasar, quizzically.

"I promised him he would have his horse before lunch." Quasar hoped this would not make him late.

"His lunch time or our lunch time?" asked Gannon, impishly.

"What do you mean?" asked Quasar.

"We do not all eat at the same time," answered Falcon with a smile. "What my brother means," he continued, playfully bumping his shoulder into Gannon, "is that in camp, food is being prepared and served at almost all hours of the day and night."

Gannon smiled. Calling for a young apprentice, he took the reins in hand.

"Please return this horse to Sage," said Gannon, handing the reins to the boy. "He's Sky Blue."

"Right away, my lord," answered the lad, who immediately left at a brisk trot.

Falcon led the group toward the main pavilion.

"I'm glad you remembered the horse," said Falcon as they walked.

"Me too," answered Quasar politely.

"I mean, for Sage's sake," said Falcon.

"Oh?" remarked Nemo.

"Yes. You promised to have it back by lunch. He would not have eaten lunch until you returned the horse. To do otherwise would be to break your promise," continued Falcon.

"I don't understand," said Quasar.

"It is a thing of honor. Your honor. He would rather go hungry than allow you to be dishonored."

Quasar stood quietly for a moment. "Your men serve you well," he said, respectfully.

Just then the party was met by a beautiful woman. Her eyes were like pools of ebony; deep, endless. She wore a white gown with red trim. Her waist length black hair shimmered with every movement of her head. It was tied back by a thin red ribbon. Falcon's face glowed with joy at first sight of her.

"May I present to you my wife, Cilantra," announced Falcon formally. "Cilantra, these are friends of my father," said Falcon pausing momentarily, "and of Gannon and me," he continued warmly. "Nemo, Lord of Silverglade, and his Counsel, Lord Quasar."

Quasar and Nemo bowed deeply. Cilantra smiled and extended her hand.

"I have heard of your visit. And of the beautiful Silverglade," said Falcon's wife. Her voice was as sweet as winter roses, her smile dazzling white. "I am very pleased to meet you."

Quasar and Nemo were stunned by her beauty. Turning to her husband, she continued, "Your father asked me to find you. He will not be able to join you for lunch. Duty leads him elsewhere."

"It often happens these days," said Falcon to Quasar and Nemo. "We'll just have to eat without him."

"The Lord Hiram expressly asked that I extend his apologies to you," Cilantra said to Quasar and Nemo.

"Of course," said Quasar smiling back at Falcon's wife. Nemo was silent, too intimidated to speak.

"Lord Falcon, may I speak to you," asked Cilantra quietly. By this, of course, she meant to speak in private. The two stepped a few feet away. She whispered for a moment, and a smile eclipsed his face.

"My dear Cilantra, and the other wives, have taken this opportunity to plan a family lunch by the grove. Our children are playing there already."

Falcon pointed to a dense grove of trees not far from the main camp.

"Do you mind?" he asked Quasar and Nemo.

"We would love it!" said Quasar and Nemo together. In truth, they had not looked forward to another meal eaten in silence.

Falcon took Cilantra's hand in his own, and the group walked to the grove. Lunch was already in progress. Lord Vine had worked quickly and set up tables and benches and large soft cloths on the ground. In the absence of the Lord Hiram, formality was banned.

The House of Hiram was close. He had raised his sons to love one another. At this meal there was laughter and joking. No rivalries were evident. These men honored one another's successes and laughed at their own failures. Today they talked of their mother Queen Elisa, their sister Lady Casandra, their home and strategies of war.

After lunch Quasar and Nemo watched Falcon play with his own twin sons. They felt a profound longing for their own lost families.

"When it comes time for me to marry and have children," said Nemo quietly to Quasar. "I could hope for none better than this."

"We must pray that it be so," replied Quasar solemnly.

As the day progressed Quasar was reminded of their task. He pushed the thought away as often as it came. Finally, he motioned to his friend.

"Nemo!" he called loudly, "I'm afraid it is time to go home."

Nemo turned and stared silently at Quasar. Then, as if suddenly waking up from a wonderful dream, he nodded his head slowly.

"You're right," he agreed. "As it is, we'll have to hurry to make it back by nightfall."

With some protest, Gannon guided Quasar and Nemo back to their tent.

By the time Quasar and Nemo had changed into their own clothes, their horses had been saddled and brought to the tent. Falcon joined them and his brother.

"I'm sorry you have to leave so soon," said Gannon in simple sincerity. "Falcon and I can't even ride with you," he added sadly.

"We too, have duties," said Falcon. "Perhaps you will return soon?"

"Yes, or perhaps you can visit us?" said Nemo.

"Our homes are always open to you," added Quasar.

"Thank you," said Falcon smiling first at

Gannon, and then to Quasar and Nemo. "One of my men will see you safely to the King's Highway."

Falcon motioned to a red uniformed man waiting nearby on horseback.

"Farewell, Nemo, Lord of Silverglade. Farewell, Lord Quasar." The four shook hands without further words.

As they left the compound, Quasar and Nemo and their escort happened upon Hogan, the guard. He looked up from his post, but, recognizing them, quickly lowered his eyes.

"You there. Are you not Hogan?" shouted Nemo. Quasar was again surprised by Nemo's boldness.

"Yes, sir, I am."

"Is it well with you, Hogan?" asked Nemo.

"Yes, sir!" answered the guard, smartly. His grin was full and shameless.

"Is it well with your Captain?" asked Nemo.

"Yes, sir. It is very well with Captain Balworth, sir." After a moment's thought, Hogan continued, "And, thank you, sir!"

Nemo was genuinely surprised. "For what, Hogan?"

"It had to be you, sir. Today, the Lord Hiram took the mid-day meal with us." Hogan paused, and continued humbly. "When the meal was over, he promoted me, sir. The Lord Hiram himself made me a full Lieutenant. Thank you, sir, for your kind words."

Nemo smiled. "You said it yourself, Lieutenant Hogan. The Lord Hiram made you a Lieutenant, not I. Serve him well."

"Yes, sir. I shall serve him well, indeed."

CHAPTER 5
The Road Home

*A*fter bidding farewell to Lieutenant Hogan, Quasar and Nemo found themselves on the road home. Though they would never forget their time with the House of Hiram, Quasar and Nemo felt a refreshing freedom, now that they were shepherds again. They rode on in silent contemplation. Much had taken place in such a short time.

Without warning, Quasar slapped Nemo on the back.

"Well Nemo, Lord of Silverglade," laughed Quasar. "I'll race you to the First Bridge."

Nemo kicked his horse and the race was on. The pair exploded joyously down the road, even crossing the bridges at full gallop.

By sunset, Quasar and Nemo reached a familiar fork in the road. The right fork led to their ranches, the other, uphill to Silverglade. Nemo stopped his horse.

"Quasar," said Nemo, his voice dark as a

moonless night. "I am not going home tonight. I must spend the night in Silverglade. Will you come with me?"

It was rare that either Quasar or Nemo ever denied a request from the other, but tonight, Quasar longed for his own ranch. The road to Silverglade was longer than the road home and the sun had already set. They had traveled non-stop since leaving Falcon and Gannon. Quasar looked at his friend a long time before answering. Nemo's face and voice were creased in worry.

"If you'd like," Quasar said finally, his smile and cheerful tone a conscious effort. "Besides, you owe me breakfast. You lost the race."

Nemo did not move. His thoughts had darkened.

"I shouldn't have left them alone," he said, suddenly.

"Who?' asked Quasar.

"My sheep, of course," answered Nemo, "What do you think we are talking about?" Nemo seemed annoyed. He was worried.

"I thought we were talking about breakfast," answered Quasar, smiling to himself. "You asked me to spend the night in Silverglade so you could make me breakfast in the morning. Remember?" Quasar hoped to lighten Nemo's mood.

"I'm going to Silverglade because that's where I left my sheep when we went to town," said Nemo. "I thought we would be back the same day," he continued, more to himself than to Quasar. He was mad at himself for putting his sheep in danger.

"I shouldn't have left them alone," he said again

Quasar thought for a moment, before speaking.

"You could have hired shepherds, like I did," said Quasar, carefully.

They had had this conversation a dozen times. It was the one thing on which they disagreed. Quasar was a good shepherd, but he saw the sheep as a business. He had hired-men to handle the day-to-day care of his flocks. Nemo, on the other hand, found it hard to let others care for his flocks. He did have hired helpers, but Nemo often stayed in the fields with them and his sheep. Sometimes, he alone stood watch over his flocks at night, especially when they grazed in Silverglade.

"You're right," said Nemo after a long pause.

This surprised Quasar. He looked at his friend, wondering if he was joking, but Nemo's face was hard as stone. There was no humor in it. He was sorry that Nemo was so worried. Quasar prayed silently that nothing had happened to Nemo's sheep.

Fortunately, Nemo had left his flocks grazing in Silverglade. The sheep were usually safe there. Tonight, however, Nemo took no comfort in his dear Silverglade. He worried that the shadowy Evil might have returned. He rode in silence, nursing his fears, hoping against hope that his last campsite would be undisturbed.

Several hours later, they reached the campsite. Quasar returned thanks to God when he heard the soft contented bleating of the sheep and the bark of Nemo's dog. He lit a fire and began preparations for the night.

Nemo found his sheep exactly where he had left them. Still, he did not rest. In the darkness he took time to survey the sheep, touching them. After reassuring himself that all was well, Nemo joined Quasar at the campfire. They ate a light dinner and quickly fell asleep.

Quasar slept deeply and peacefully. Nemo, however, saw the stars flicker and disappear, once again. Again he felt The Evil.

"NO! NO!" he cried loudly.

Nemo's screaming shocked Quasar awake. He stumbled toward the sound. Nemo was standing a dozen paces away, protecting his head with his arms. Quasar quickly scanned the heavens. He could see nothing but glorious stars. He ran to his friend.

"Nemo, Nemo, wake up," shouted Quasar. "It's a dream. You're dreaming," he cried as he shook Nemo awake.

Nemo stopped fighting as his eyes jerked open. It was some time before he could speak. He could not describe the dream.

"It was The Evil," repeated Nemo over and over. "It was The Evil."

Quasar looked Nemo full in the face and whispered, "The evil we face may be great, but we shall prevail." At that very moment, the sun announced the dawn.

CHAPTER 6
Gravefire

$\mathcal{B}$y the time Nemo had the fire going, Quasar returned with five beautiful fish, cleaned and ready to cook. Nemo knew where wild onions grew. There is nothing quite as good as ponta caught early in the day, cooked on an open fire with onions, and eaten while the dew is still on the ground. Bread from Nemo's pouch and water from the lake completed a perfect breakfast.

"Even the wealthy eat no better then this," said Nemo, thinking back to the House of Hiram.

"And few eat this well," answered Quasar. The time spent with Falcon and Gannon already seemed unreal to Quasar.

Nemo smiled slightly, thinking of his dream. He had acted like a child. His screams had even frightened the sheep. And yet, it had seemed so real. Nemo did not know what it meant, if anything, but he was sure The Evil was no dream. No matter what came, Nemo knew he and Quasar would face it together.

"When we are done here, I have something to show you," said Quasar, his voice quiet and hard. "We can leave the sheep with your dog. They'll be fine."

Nemo looked at Quasar. His expression was blank, emotionless, his eyes narrowed in thought.

"What is it?" asked Nemo.

No answer.

"Where is it?"

Again, no answer.

"Quasar, what are you talking about?"

Still Quasar didn't answer.

"All right, what aren't you talking about?" insisted Nemo.

Quasar looked at his friend for a long time before he spoke.

"I know how our parents died," he said simply, and then walked down the path to the lake.

Nemo was speechless as he followed Quasar. The death of their families was a mystery, one that even now ate away at his heart.

It had happened down the mountain. *What could Quasar have possibly learned about their deaths here,* wondered Nemo.

Few of their friends ever spoke of it, now. And if they did, they were careful. No one ever mentioned it at night. Some, out of superstition or respect, extinguished any candle or open flame before mentioning that terrible night. It was a tragedy beyond imagination and beyond reason. *Why bring it up today?* thought Nemo.

Both of the boys had lost farm and family to fire. The families and the livestock had all burned to death. The farms were totally consumed by fire; a fire, some said, with a mind of its own.

The ranches were ajacent to each other, as they still are today, with miles of land between the ranch houses. It was the houses, the barns and all that was in them that burned. The forest and fields between the ranches did not burn. That was part of the mystery.

Quasar and Nemo would have died with the others, but they had gone riding at dusk. On a whim, they spent the night in Silverglade. This whim had saved their lives. It also cursed them with unanswered questions. Nemo repeated the questions he had asked himself a thousand times:

What had started the fires?

Why did both farms burn, miles apart, on the same night?

How is it that no one survived?

These questions were never answered. Some said wind had carried embers, but the boys knew the night had been calm. They had stayed up late in Silverglade, stargazing, talking and enjoying the night, all while their loved ones died. It was not the wind.

There were other questions too, questions even Quasar and Nemo no longer spoke, no longer thought. But, in silence, the rumors lived. Few knew the full story.

In the eternity of a thought, Nemo relived the awful details of that morning. Coming home he first discovered the remains of three bodies. Each was away from any of the ranch buildings. They should not have burned. These three men should have lived.

Nemo had found his cousin first, on the gate road, with the carcass of a saddled horse.

At first he didn't even know what it was. Then he refused to believe what it was. In horror he had rushed to the ranch house and found the other two, one near a well, the other near the entrance to a root cellar. All should have been safe. All were trying to escape; by horse, by water, by cellar. All had been burned beyond belief. Stumbling onward, Nemo had found his parents and the others.

Images of the smoldering dead flashed in and out of his mind. He struggled to clear his thoughts as he joined Quasar at the lake. They stood silently at the water's edge. Quasar stared out across a narrow inlet.

"I was fishing here, this morning, when I saw it," Quasar said quietly.

Nemo followed his gaze. There in the distance was the stand of oak that marked the resting place of their loved ones. Through a blur of tears, Nemo remembered scattering the ashes of his mother, father, sisters, aunt and uncles. Quasar, too, had done the same for his family.

Nemo could see nothing new, nothing strange, nothing but the beautiful trees and the lush grass.

"Quasar?" Nemo's weakened voice broke the silence. "Quasar, what do you see?" Nemo could barely speak.

Quasar pointed to the stand of oak.

"Look at the grass," he answered firmly. "Can't you see it!" It was more a command than a question.

Nemo gazed at the trees and then at the grass. Both appeared as they always did, beautiful, peaceful, serene. Nemo could see nothing out of the ordinary. Then, just as he was about to ask again, his mind seemed to focus.

He could see it. Incredible! Was it really there? Yes! As he continued to stare in silence it became all the more clear.

How can this be? screamed Nemo's mind, but his voice barely whispered, "How?"

There on the ground, formed by thickly growing grasses and shadows from the oaks, was the heinous image of a great winged dragon. Its talons were clutching the white rocks that marked the grave site. Even fire-breath was there, formed by yellow, orange, and red wild flowers.

"How?" repeated Nemo.

"I don't know," answered Quasar harshly. "I don't understand, yet. But, The Evil must die. If some flying worm has killed my family and friends, I shall find it and rid the land of it forever. Its friends shall die and I shall kill its young. If this grasshopper has burned my house I shall take its house, and all that is in it."

Quasar spoke strangely, strongly, prophetically.

Nemo was confused. He had never seen Quasar like this before. Gone was the face of his boyhood friend. In its place was the face of a warrior; solemn, set, determined.

"What are you saying?" asked Nemo. "I see the dragon. But what does it mean?"

Quasar didn't answer his friend. He stood facing the dragon, wind blowing his blond hair wildly. A thousand thoughts circled his head. He heard voices, remembered long forgotten scenes. Details, like threads in a tapestry, came together. Quasar stood transfixed, lost in a swamp of revelation and emotion. Finally, Nemo's voice penetrated his fog.

"Why are you so sure the dragon is real?

What has this to do with our families?"

Nemo didn't really want answers. He wanted to forget. He wanted to ignore.

Slowly, Quasar returned to the now. His speech was labored, one word at a time. His looks frightened Nemo.

"She would have killed you and me if we had been home." Quasar's voice began to rise with his passion. His pace quickened.

"Think about it," he commanded. "All the mysteries are solved," he shouted to the sky. "All the questions are answered!" His voice echoed throughout Silverglade. Quasar paused for a moment. He looked back to the dragon in the grass. Then his head dropped slowly. When he spoke again, his voice was soft and calm.

"I think, somehow, our families are speaking from their graves."

"You sound like an old woman," said Nemo as he turned to leave.

"My grandmother was an old woman," answered Quasar sharply. Then slowly, deliberately, he added, "And she burned, too."

Nemo stopped. Grandmother Tata had loved others more than her ownself. She loved everyone in deed and in heart. "Only love replaces pains, only love in truth remains," was her answer for every problem. Her love was so well known that her name had come to mean something like "kindness without measure". To be called "tata", now, was a great compliment.

"Don't you remember the stories she told us of her mother's childhood. The burnings. The fighting. Stories of a dark time, an evil time. A time when dragons came, summoned from some desolate place?"

Quasar paused, remembering how the stories frightened him as a child.

Slowly Nemo collapsed onto the grass. Faces, voices, memories, washed over him. He could say nothing, do nothing, but sit and stare at the grass image. He knew in his heart it was true.

Perhaps it was a natural thing. Perhaps the grasses grew faster, thicker, where the ashes had been spread. Or, perhaps it was forces little understood. Perhaps God was speaking. Whatever the cause, Quasar and Nemo now knew how their families had died.

How long the boys sat in silence they

couldn't tell. So many thoughts, so many questions, so much went unsaid.

What are we to do?

How can we avenge our families?

Is revenge the reason for this revelation? No, not revenge.

If the good do not oppose evil, who will?

Suddenly, Nemo cried out, "My sheep!"

Quasar, startled as if from sleep, jumped to his feet and began to run toward the hillside where sheep grazed peacefully.

Again Nemo shouted, "Quasar, my sheep. Look Quasar, my sheep."

Quasar looked back at his friend. Nemo wasn't facing his sheep, he was running toward the graves, toward the dragon, toward their past, toward their future.

"Can't you see it?" shouted Nemo as he ran. "The dragon has my sheep. She's got two of my sheep!"

Quasar suddenly saw it. There, in the claws of that awful flying worm, were two sheep; white grave markers really, but in the morning light, they somehow looked like sheep.

Without speaking, both boys knew: This

was no mere cry for revenge. This was a cry of warning. The love of their families was reaching out from the ground and warning them of danger, evil; warning them that their lives, and the lives of all their friends, were at risk.

CHAPTER 7
Trapped

$\mathcal{I}$n the twilight all seemed peaceful, quiet, serene. The evening meal was cooking on the campfire. Its aroma filled the night sky. The forms of two shepherds could still be seen in the fading rose of sunset. Soon, however, they would only be silhouettes around the fire. Sheep peacefully slept nearby. All was perfectly calm. Too perfect. Too calm.

If one watched long and carefully enough one could see that some things were not right. The shepherds never moved, not even to cook their meal. They never spoke, never ate. They didn't breathe. The food was too far from the fire to really cook. It was close enough to warm and give off scent, but that was all. The sheep closest to the fire also didn't move, they couldn't; ropes around their necks and hindquarters staked them to the ground.

And too, only a novice would camp this close to the tall woods in Silverglade. Sheep like open lands. This tiny glade was surrounded by old, deep woods; woods that would offer a perfect hiding place for wolves or anything else that wanted to remain unseen. Quasar had counted on it. He had chosen this place himself.

All day long he and Nemo had planned and worked. They sensed The Evil would return tonight, and they had to be ready.

Stunned at first by the morning's revelation, they had been moved to action by the unexpected death of a young hawk. Diving for fish, the hawk had been greedy. It had taken two large fish at once. The weight of the fish combined with the height of the woods proved too great for the immature bird. He had released one fish and then the other, but too late to clear the trees, too late to land, too late even to perch. All he could do was cry out in rage. With a wing broken by a branch, the hawk fell to his death. Together, Quasar and Nemo had vowed to bring this same fate upon the dragon.

While Quasar built the camp, formed and dressed the life-sized "shepherds," and staked the sheep, Nemo searched the woods for just the right branches. Then, as his friend tied nets and sacks of rocks to the sheep, Nemo sat down to work the branches into bow and arrows. Nemo thought of Lord Shank and his archers. He silently prayed that his aim tonight would be as true as it had been the day before.

Quickly his fingers moved, weaving string, carving shaft, curing bow. Other workers would have taken weeks. Nemo had only hours. In that short time he made two fine bows and six stone tipped arrows. It would have to be enough.

The plan was simple. Lure the dragon to the glade by the light of the fire and the scent of food. Entice her to take one sheep, or better yet two. She would be surprised. The rocks and nets would work together. Each of the sheep would be heavy to lift and impossible to release.

"The trees," Quasar explained, "will do double work." He had chosen this place because it was small.

"First," Quasar continued, "The trees will slow the dragon's descent. She can't enter the glade quickly because it is too small and the trees are too tall. Her decent will be steep and slow."

A strange glow filled Quasar's eyes as he spoke.

"Then, weighted by the sheep and rocks the trees will block her escape. She might even crash into them like the hawk." Quasar smiled at the idea. "The arrows will finish her off."

Nemo had never seen Quasar so confident.

All was now ready. Quasar and Nemo waited silently. They were hidden by trees, boulders and underbrush. Each scanned the night sky, waiting for movement, a shadow, anything that would warn them that the dragon was near. Only their eyes moved.

Quasar had repeated his warning all day: "No talking, no moving, no shooting, until the dragon is close enough to smell."

The bows were strong and the arrows sharp, but to pierce the dragon's scaled hide Quasar and Nemo would have to shoot when she was but a few feet away. They agreed that the first arrows would fly as she grabbed the sheep. It was dangerous, but surprise was their ally. They assured themselves that the weight of the rocks would slow her ascent long enough for another arrow or two.

The wait was long. The sheep slept. The fire was now just glowing embers. Twice Nemo had wanted to add wood to make the fire bright; twice Quasar's eyes flashed warning. Now, Nemo found it almost impossible to stay awake.

The words had been forming in his mind for sometime. Nemo felt he had to tell his friend they had failed. The night was too long, too quiet. The dragon, he was sure, was not coming.

Just as Nemo's doubt was about to find its voice the stars overhead flickered and disappeared. Evil prickled the hairs on his neck. The dragon had come.

Nemo glanced at Quasar, who already had shaft on string. They both watched as the shadow silently circled overhead. Her wings didn't move. She made no sound. The sheep were still unaware that their death descended.

Nemo's mind was now amazingly clear. Twice he saw the white underbelly of the thing. Twice he stopped himself from shooting, from springing the trap too soon. He held one arrow at the ready and a second clenched in his bow hand. They would fly to kill the beast. Everything slowed. *Wait! Patience! Not yet,* Nemo silently reminded himself. He wondered what his friend was thinking.

Quasar stood stone faced. He had but one thought, one vision, one intent. When his arrow flew it would pierce the dragon's heart. His mind focused on that one thing. Nothing else existed.

From above, the dragon viewed the glade, jeweled with glowing ruby embers. She circled as she descended. It would not be an easy kill. The dragon could see that the trees were tall and thickly clustered. She thought for a moment of finding easier prey, but her pride refused. This little obstacle would not stop her. She was, after all, old and skilled. She enjoyed the challenge.

Circling, she tested the winds, measured the tree tops, planned her entrance and exit. Yes, this was a treat. It would be a thing to remember and relish and recount. There is but one thing dragons love more than gold. Themselves. Pride is at their very core. They love to boast of their own achievements.

Besting one another in tales of strength and cunning is a favorite dragon pastime. This verbal dance is the centerpiece of Dragonfest. Once or twice each century dragons, the world over, assemble. Ancient rituals usher adolescent fledglings into adulthood. Contests of speed in flight and of strength in battle are held. Above all else there is the telling and retelling of stories. It is an oral history in which the teller is always the hero.

This kill, thought the dragon with a chuckle, *will make a fun little story.*

Quasar and Nemo noticed a momentary glow from her nostrils. The boys watched, dry mouthed, as the dragon cleared the tree tops. Wings extended, talons open, her strength and grace were awesome. It seemed impossible that something so huge and heavy could actually float. It was as if she hovered over the camp. Bows fully drawn, Quasar and Nemo waited for her to trip the snare.

Panic seized the sheep. Those who were free ran bleating. Those staked for sacrifice kicked helplessly. Suddenly, the dragon dropped and firmly grabbed its victims, one in each talon.

Quasar and Nemo gasped in shock. It was not as they had planned. The rocks and nets were useless. She ignored the sheep and grabbed the forms of the shepherds!

Time raced. Quasar and Nemo had to act

quickly. There were no nets to entangle the dragon, no rocks to slow her ascent. There was no extra weight at all. The shepherd forms were made of old clothes stuffed with leaves and twigs. If the boys had really camped out, they would have died in their sleep. She was not hunting food, she was hunting them!

The dragon was momentarily confused. She had expected something else.

Was this a trick? she thought. *No, a trap!*

It was all too clear. Enraged, she screeched and whirled in mid-flight. Quasar got off the first shot, but it glanced off a wing. Nemo, anticipating her turn, waited a moment and then shot sure and true. Both of his arrows struck the dragon, but, she was too far away. The arrows did no harm, but they told the dragon all she needed to know. In a moment, the glade was consumed in fire.

❧ ❧ ❧ ❧ ❧

Captain Lewis laughed again at his good fortune. Here he was stationed in an island paradise. A secret island at that, with plenty of sweet water and all the provisions anyone would ever need. In addition, he was with the best army in the world.

His cabin boy, the Schooper lad, was recovering well. One of the best healers in the world had seen to that. The captain had become attached to the boy. He wanted to make sure his first mate's son was brought to full health again. Burns are dangerous and children are so easily lost.

Lewis felt he could stay here forever. He smiled at the thought. Only one thing would be better. If his dear Elena and their own son Tod were here with him, but alas, they were gone. The pox had seen to that. Such a long, ugly death. It left him hollow inside.

Captain Lewis took a deep breath and looked around. After spending most of the night visiting the healing tent he had decided to take the healer's advice.

"Don't stay here again all day," said the kindly old woman. "Get some good air. Climb the mountain. Explore the island. It will do you good."

So, Captain Lewis found himself on the trail to the Top of the World, as it was called. It was not yet dawn, but no matter, the trail was well marked. Besides, the darkness added a greater challenge

It had been an invigorating climb. Steep in some parts, but not too hard. Just what he needed. He stopped from time to time, enjoying the night and the stars. Before he realized it he was at the crest. The view from the top was grand, even at night.

From this rocky cliff he could see the fires and lights of the entire camp-town. He could also see his harbor, the one in which Fyrmatus was anchored. By looking down the other side of the cliff he could see the harbor on the opposite side of the island, too. Almost half the fleet was anchored in the other bay as he thought of it.

Settling himself against a huge banana tree he closed this eyes and awaited sunrise. He never noticed the huge banana spider that crawled out of the tree near his head. As he dozed the first rays of dawn kissed the clouds and made them blush.

"You'd love it here, Elena," said Captain Lewis, yawning out loud. He allowed his dream to stay a moment longer.

"The air is sea-fresh, the water clear, the

evenings mild."

As he spoke he picked a wondrous red and yellow bloom. He held it to his nose and breathed deeply.

"And the flowers, ah, you would fill our house with fresh flowers every day. You'd love it here, Elena," he said again, then crushed the flower and dropped it. His dream was gone.

◌ ◌ ◌ ◌ ◌

Nemo stood, transfixed, unable to move or to think. His shots had been perfect. What had gone wrong? Why didn't the dragon die?

Quasar shook Nemo. "We must run or burn!" he shouted.

Pulling Nemo into a run, Quasar guided the pair deeper into the woods. They moved none too soon. The place where they had stood was engulfed in flame. Fortunately for them, the dragon could only guess where they were hidden. Blinded by rage, she randomly blasted the forest.

Nemo suddenly stopped running. His head was cocked to one side, unseeing, listening.

"We can't stop here. Keep moving,"

commanded Quasar.

"No!" shouted Nemo. "She will see us, and we will die. Come this way."

Quasar changed course and followed Nemo down a narrow path. It took them to a pond at the base of a small waterfall. Near the falls was a large outcropping of stone.

Without hesitation, Quasar and Nemo jumped into the cold water. They swam to the rock and hid.

"I have never seen this place," said Quasar.

"Silverglade has many secrets," answered Nemo. "We must be quiet and watch. The dragon will not give up easily."

Before Quasar could answer, the woods around the pond burst into flames. The dragon came from above, raking the mountain, the waterfall, and the pond with flame.

Instinctively the boys held their breath and disappeared underwater. Protected by stone and water, they survived. When they surfaced, they were boys no longer. They had aged in a baptism of fire.

CHAPTER 8
Secrets of Silverglade

$\mathcal{T}$wice, as the forest fire died down, the dragon returned to again strafe the area with flame. She hovered and circled above, silently watching for any sign of life. For the boys, the wet, cold wait continued. Choking smoke covered the little pond. Heat from the fire radiated along the surface of the fridged water.

Slowly, the smoke cleared and the heat subsided. At long last Quasar and Nemo felt safe enough to come out of hiding. Aching and numb from the cold water, they cautiously swam out from under their rocky shield. In the gradual silence that came as the fires died, they carefully climbed ashore.

Shivering with cold, skin wrinkled from hours in the dark icy water, the two stood and stared. The damage was beyond words. The air was still thick with smoke. Everything they could see through the haze was burned. Even the rocks were charred black. Without thinking, they both moved to a stump that still burned.

Nemo laughed a little. "At least we have heat," he mumbled. Nothing more was said.

Quasar and Nemo stood rubbing their arms and legs, trying to get warm. Their wet, dripping clothes made pools of muddy soot around their feet. Nemo noticed his shephard's cloak was singed. The dragon fire had come very close indeed."I don't know why I just stood there," said Nemo quietly. He ran his fingers lightly over his blackened left shoulder. "I am alive because of you, Quasar."

"And I'm alive because of you," answered Quasar, trying to sound lighthearted.

Nemo shook his head, but said nothing.

"You knew about this pond," continued Quasar. "You're the one who first dove into the water." He felt sure that Nemo had saved their lives. "You led us under the rock. I just followed."

Quasar was right. Nemo had guided the pair to stand, chin deep in water, under a long, flat, stone shelf. This had protected them from the onslaught of the demon breath. It also gave them precious little view of what was taking place. For a long time all they knew was that fire raged around them.

"Don't you remember?" asked Nemo. "I tried to swim out. You pulled me back."

Nemo shuddered as his mind felt the heat of the flames again. He could see himself just beginning to swim out from under the rock as fiery death hovered above. Fortunately, Quasar caught a glimpse of dark movement. He pulled Nemo back as fire exploded on the stone shelf above their heads. Had they moved out a moment or two earlier, both would have died.

"Well, that helped me too," said Quasar closing his eyes to block his thoughts. "It gave me patience to stay in the cold water."

Now the warmth from the burning stump, though welcome at first, brought intense pain. Their deadened nerves revived. Signaling displeasure at the abuse they had endured, their arms and legs shivered, ached and cramped.

"We must move on," said Quasar. Nemo only groaned his assent.

By the eerie light of countless small fires, Quasar and Nemo made their way toward what had been the glade. This waking was worse than any dream. The devastation was complete. Slowly, they made it back to the sight of their trap. Even the ground and rocks were black and melted.

"Look. Look," cried Quasar.

"I know," said Nemo shaking his head sadly. "Silverglade is gone. It is all gone. Burned. I can't believe it."

"No," shouted Quasar excitedly. "Look. Look." He pointed up through giant skeletons of scorched trees.

Amazingly, two hundred paces away, the forest was intact. Through a haze of smoke, Quasar and Nemo stared at the tall trees, the lush ferns and undergrowth of the old forest. It was completely untouched by flame.

"I can't believe it," roared Quasar.

"Thank you. Oh, thank you," prayed Nemo as he stumbled to the ebonied edge of the forest. It was as if he were standing between life and death.

On one side all was green and alive; on the other everything was blackened and dead. Nemo sat on a rock at the very edge of the burn. It was still warm and covered with a moss-like ash.

"This is better than I hoped," said Nemo.

He stretched out his arm and gently grabbed a living fern. Its edges were slightly curled and brown from heat, but it had survived. He held the plant to his face breathing deeply its earthy scent.

What an awesome creature this dragon was! From within the inferno, it had seemed that all the world was aflame. Now they knew that the dragon was selective in her destructive vengeance.

"Can dragons really be that keen?" asked Nemo quietly. Quasar had no answer.

Dazed and weak the two pressed through the thick greenery of the forest. What had been a welcomed sight moments before was now an obstacle. Branches that would not normally hinder them were now challenges to the exhausted pair. Thorns and thickets that should be mere irritants now were roadblocks. They were miles from the road. They needed food and warmth.

Nemo stopped for a moment. His head dropped, he stood still and then fell suddenly to the ground. The upper half of his body crashed through some low-growing bushes.

"Nemo, are you all right?" asked Quasar. Nemo didn't answer. Grabbing his friend's legs and shaking them, Quasar shouted, "Nemo, you can't give up!"

Nemo answered in muffled grunts that Quasar could not understand. Panic rose within him. He must not let his friend die.

"Nemo, come on. Stand up. You've got to stand up!"

Nemo slowly lifted his head out from under the bush. Red oozed from the corner of his mouth. Quasar saw that his entire face was smeared red.

"Why stand up?" asked Nemo, as his face broke into a full smile. "These berries are ripe and sweet."

He handed Quasar a huge red juzzberry. Moonlight glistened on its ripe succulent pulp.

"I don't know about you, but I'm starved," laughed Nemo, eyes full of mischief.

Nemo thrust his head back into the bush and once again began eating berries.

Quasar stood for a moment, unable to make sense of it. Without thinking he popped the berry into his mouth. A trickle of red liquid colored his chin. Energized by the sweet juice, Quasar laughed out loud. Red droplets flew through the air, catapulted by his laughter. Quasar watched the drops land near Nemo's feet. In another moment he joined his friend, picking berries with both hands. They ate all they could find.

"These are the best berries I've ever tasted," laughed Quasar.

Nemo just kept eating. Strengthened by this lush winter fruit, the boys lay down on soft moss to rest and wait for dawn. They stretched their aching legs, flexed their ankles, wiggled their frozen toes.

"You know," said Nemo, "These juzzberries just might have saved our lives."

He picked another berry. Turning it gently in his fingers, Nemo examined the bumpy crimson surface before dropping it into his mouth. Using his tongue, Nemo slowly crushed the berry against the roof of his mouth. Deliciously sweet liquid exploded across his taste buds.

Nemo closed his eyes contentedly. His thoughts turned to home. A long sigh escaped from his bright scarlet lips.

"Listen," whispered Quasar, alarm sounding in his voice.

"I think when we get home I'm going to

plant some juzzberry bushes right next to the house," continued Nemo, deaf to his friend's concern. "Then I can have berries all winter long."

"Be quiet," whispered Quasar. "Listen, something is coming!"   Nemo heard the sound too, and sat straight up. He forgot about planting bushes, forgot about berries, forgot about everything else. Once again his mind froze in terror. If the dragon found them here, they would not survive. There was nothing to offer protection here, no water to cool the fire, no monolith to shield them from fiery blasts. Their only hope was to hide. Silently, they slipped under the thick juzzberry bush, and waited. They didn't wait long.

Something large pushed noisily through the ferns right next to where the boys hid. It stopped right were they had laid, moments before. They could not see it, but they could hear it breathing, they could even feel its body heat.

I wonder if the dragon has a good sense of smell? thought Nemo. How could she, he said to himself, *with all that fire and smoke in her nose?*

Quasar carefully moved a branch and peered out. "We should have stayed near the pond," he thought. He looked up directly onto the underbelly of the beast. It stood over them, not a foot away. Slowly he reached for his long-knife.

Maybe I can stab her heart, he thought desperately.

His fingers touched his belt as he felt blindly for the blade. Quasar scanned the beast for a weak point. Its double chests, heaving in unison, were covered in short hair-like fur, not scales. *Everyone says that dragons are covered in snaky scales. They're all wrong,* thought Quasar. *I supposed, few have been close enough to really see a dragon...* Quasar swallowed hard at his next thought: *...and lived to tell what they saw.* He couldn't help wonder if they would live to tell about this one.

Slowly, Quasar lowered himself deeper into the bush.

"If we can stay hidden long enough," whispered Quasar, "perhaps she will fly away and look somewhere else."

Nemo had the good sense to slowly, silently nod an answer. From his place in the bushes Quasar could only see the animal's legs. They were much thinner than he expected.

Wait! thought Quasar. His mind began to clear.

Two, Four. He began counting the legs. Slowly he turned his head. *Four, six, no, eight legs!*

"It isn't a dragon!" whispered Quasar.

"Are you sure?" asked Nemo.

Quasar nodded.

"Then, what is it?" asked Nemo, who could only hear the thing breathe.

Quasar peered from the bushes. Slowly, he stood and stepped from his hiding place. Nemo lost sight of him.

"Quasar?" whispered Nemo. Nemo heard no answer. "Quasar?" he repeated slightly louder. Still nothing.

A branch snapped. The animal snorted and stamped. Then the forest erupted in laughter. Cautiously, Nemo looked out from his hiding place. There was Quasar, bent in laughter, holding the reins of not one, but two horses. Their own horses. Somehow, both their horses had also survived.

"Nemo," chided Quasar. "You didn't unsaddle these poor animals."

"Me?" answered Nemo as he stepped from the bushes. "I thought you were supposed to do it." Nemo felt confused.

"I did it last time. It was your turn," laughed Quasar.

In all of their preparations as they hurried to trap the dragon, the boys had forgotten the first rule of good horsemanship: 'Always care for your horse.' Because of their carelessness, not only had the horses survived, but also here they stood, fully saddled and ready to ride.

Having run away at the first sign of the dragon, the horses had long since calmed down. They were idly grazing in the forest, waiting for Quasar and Nemo. The boys quickly checked them for injuries. None.

"Look here," shouted Quasar. "Our saddlebags are still full. So are the packs!"

"Warm clothes. All I want is warm clothes," chuckled Nemo as he opened his pack.

Wrapped in blankets and wearing warm dry clothes, the pair mounted their horses and headed for home. They rode slowly, carefully staying under the cover of trees. They constantly scanned the sky.

"If we see her," suggested Nemo, "we should split up and ride quickly in opposite directions."

"No," insisted Quasar, "she could still pick us off, one at a time." Then gently, he added, "Don't you remember? Your cousin burned on the gate road. He was riding a horse."

Nemo closed his eyes at the memory of finding the remains of horse and rider. It was the first body he had discovered.

"Then there is no hope," said Nemo bitterly.

"There is always hope," answered Quasar quickly. "Never give up!" he added, as much for his own benefit as for the benefit of Nemo.

"If we do see her, we just have to make sure she doesn't see us." Quasar paused for a moment, searching the dark sky. It would be light soon.

"Don't worry," he continued, truly encouraged. "I don't think God had us freeze in the water just so we could burn here. Come on." Quasar started riding again, slowly, carefully.

A few minutes later Nemo found a familiar trail. They rode in silence. A dreary exhaustion imprisoned them.

"What was that?" asked Quasar, suddenly.

"That, my friend, is sunrise," answered

Nemo.

The golden rose light encouraged him. Somehow, the sunrise made Nemo feel safe. *Incredible as it seems,* he thought, *we were attacked by a dragon and survived.*

"No, listen," Quasar whispered, interrupting Nemo's thoughts.

"Please, Quasar," said Nemo. "I've had enough for one day. I don't want to hear anything, I don't want to see anything. I just want to go home."

Quasar stopped his horse. "I'm sure I heard something," he said.

Nemo stopped riding The hair on his neck prickled as his eyes scanned the morning sky.

Please, not again. Please, please, not again, prayed Nemo silently. Then they both heard it, near and clear.

∞   ∞   ∞   ∞   ∞

A flash of motion caught Captain Lewis' eye. A hawk, which he had watch circling, suddenly turned and dived. In a second she folded her wings, falling, flying faster and faster to the kill.

Lewis strained his eyes to see the prey. At first, he could see nothing, but then, following the hawk's line of flight he saw it; a pigeon coming in from the sea. The victim must have seen the hawk too, for she increased her speed, and at the last moment dropped and turned.

The hawk screamed in frustration, rose for a moment and turned for another pass. Too late. In that moment, the pigeon disappeared. The hawk screamed again.

"Better luck next time," shouted Captain Lewis, never guessing that he had just spoken against the House of Hiram.

Little bells on the roost signaled that another bird had arrived. The Pigeon Master stirred slightly at the sound. Turning over in bed, he mumbled something and started snoring. Johan, his apprentice, waited for the order to fetch the bird. Still the Pigeon Master slept. Finally, Johan quietly walked up the narrow wobbly stairs as he had a hundred times before. The familiar sour smell and constant monotonous cooing met him as he entered the roost. It held hundreds of birds and even more cages, but there were only a dozen gates from the outside. It was such a simple thing to find which one held the new bird, and therefore the message. What made it even easier were the little red flags. They were his idea.

When a bird landed and pushed open the little gate to enter the cage it would trip a lever. Three things would then happen, automatically: Food and water would drop into bowls for the bird, the bells would tinkle, and a marker, a little red flag, would spring up on the top of the cage that held the bird. By using food and water they trained the birds to enter the gates. Johan had added the bells and the marker. It made his job easier, and had earned him a visit from Lord Herald. What a day that was, Johan remembered with a smile.

The lad walked to the flagged cage, opened the back gate and reached in for the bird. It didn't coo or flap in protest. He held her carefully and gently smoothed her feathers. Her breathing was still heavy from her labored flight.

"You'll be fine, my beauty," he said; a phrase learned from the Pigeon Master. "You'll be fine, my beauty," he repeated.

He checked to see if the silver cylinder was

still tied to her leg. It was there and so was something else. Blood.

"You're hurt, my beauty," he said calmly. "Don't worry, Johan will fix you up. Don't worry. You'll be fine."

He removed the tiny metal cylinder from the bird's leg and carefully set it aside. Then he turned his attention to the bleeding bird.

ଔ ଔ ଔ ଔ ଔ

"I hear it, but I don't believe it," cried Nemo as he kicked his horse to a run. The boys both rode quickly toward the familiar dog bark. They emerged from the forest into rolling pasture lands. There, on a gently sloping meadow, they found the sheep. The flock was contentedly grazing, last night's nightmare forgotten already. The sheep had been rounded up by Nemo's dog, Blade. Nemo jumped from his horse and ran toward the dog.

"Blade, Blade, you're alive. You're all right!" Nemo laughed.

Blade, seeing his master run, thought Nemo wanted to play their favorite game, tag.

While Nemo frantically tried to catch him, Blade jumped in circles around and around. Finally, Blade allowed himself to be caught. Nemo hugged him, enduring a wave of licks in return. Quieting the dog, Nemo carefully ran both hands through his thick curly black hair to feel for any hidden injury. There was none, but, his singed tail told Nemo how close the dog had come to dying.

"Blade, you sly 'ole dog." Laughed Nemo. "I can't believe you made it. And, you gathered the flock, too!" Nemo silently gave thanks to God for his dog. Next to Quasar, Blade was the closest thing Nemo had to a family.

Quasar and Nemo unpacked some food from the horses.

"The dog is better with sheep than we are," said Quasar, smiling.

He watched Blade circle the sheep. The dog darted in and out of the flock, always keeping one step ahead of the sheep. Quasar smiled as a stubborn sheep tried to ignore the dog's leading. Gently, efficiently, Blade guided the wayward one back.

Without a word from Nemo, Blade assembled the flock for travel. This gave Quasar and Nemo a moment to eat a quick morning meal.

"This bread tastes a little smoky," complained Quasar, good-naturedly.

"So would you, if I hadn't found the waterfall," said Nemo with a smile.

Such amazing things had happened since the bread was baked, three days before! Thinking back to that waterfall, Quasar looked quizzically at his best friend.

"What other secrets does Silverglade hold?" he asked.

The question remained unanswered, hanging in the air like a swarm of black flies. Finally, Nemo turned to Quasar and spoke quietly.

"There are things about Silverglade even I do not know. It is a special place." He looked around at the beautiful forest, letting his mind drift back to the time before his family's death.

"No one alive today even knows how special," continued Nemo. "My father once said: "When you are old enough I will show you the Seven Secrets of Silverglade." Nemo paused and sighed. He still missed his father.

"The Seven Secrets of Silverglade?" asked Quasar eagerly. "What are they?"

"He died before he told me," Nemo answered slowly. "I have spent many days walking the fields and mountains of Silverglade, looking, listening, searching for the secrets. I think I have found most of them, but, I am not sure. There is no way to be sure. The Secrets died with Father."

Quasar was quiet. He thought he knew everything about Nemo. He felt a little surprised, a little betrayed. But, he also felt a new respect for his best friend.

"Come on, Quasar," said Nemo. "Let's get my sheep home. We can talk as we ride. I've wanted to tell you about the Secrets for a long time."

Color Key To The House of Hiram

RANK IN FAMILY	NAME	COLOR	DUTIES	MARRIED WIFE NAME
Father	Hiram	Pure White – aka – The Service of Light	Head of the House of Hiram	Married - Elisa
1st son	Falcon	Blood Red – aka – The Talons	Elite Warrior Corps	Married - Cilantra
2nd son	Tulmar	Fire Orange	Armor, Weapons, Metallurgy	Married - Blanche
3rd son	Shank	Bright Yellow	Archers, long bows & cross bows	Married - Kami
4th son	Kyler	Shimmering Silver	Cavalry and Lancers	
1st daughter	Casandra	none	Help Queen Elisa at Court, engaged to Prince Aalon	
5th son	Herald	Sky Blue	Flag-men, signal-men, messenger birds	
6th son	Norrom	Dark Blue	Navy, shipping, transportation (land & sea)	
7th son	Ram	Deep Purple	Machines of War, Catapults, Ramps, Cannon	
8th son	Vine	Wine	Supplies, Food, Drink and Logistics	
9th son	Reed	Forest Green – aka – Green Eyes	Guards, Sentries, Spys, and Internal Security	
10th son	Gannon	Striped	Sciences, Medicines, History and Arts	

948537

Made in the USA